Fenway and Hattie In the Wild

Sniff out other books by Victoria J. Coe

Fenway and Hattie

**Fenway and Hattie
and the Evil Bunny Gang**

**Fenway and Hattie
Up to New Tricks**

**Fenway and Hattie
In the Wild**

Fenway and Hattie* In the Wild

Victoria J. Coe

putnam

G. P. PUTNAM'S SONS

G. P. PUTNAM'S SONS
an imprint of Penguin Random House LLC, New York

Text copyright © 2019 by Victoria J. Coe.
Illustrations copyright © 2016 by Kristine Lombardi.

Visit us online at penguinrandomhouse.com

Library of Congress Cataloging-in-Publication Data
Names: Coe, Victoria J., author.
Title: Fenway and Hattie in the wild / Victoria J. Coe.
Description: New York: G. P. Putnam's Sons, [2019] | Series: [Fenway and Hattie; 4]
Summary: "Fenway gets a taste of the wild when he goes on a back-to-school camping trip with Hattie where they both feel nervous about being the new kid"— Provided by publisher.
Identifiers: LCCN 2018052677 (print) | LCCN 2018057368 (ebook) | ISBN 9781984812513 (ebook) | ISBN 9781984812506 (hardback)
Subjects: | CYAC: Jack Russell terrier—Fiction. | Dogs—Fiction. | Camping—Fiction. | Human-animal relationships—Fiction. | BISAC: JUVENILE FICTION / Animals / Dogs. | JUVENILE FICTION / Humorous Stories. | JUVENILE FICTION / Sports & Recreation / Camping & Outdoor Activities.
Classification: LCC PZ7.1.C635 (ebook) | LCC PZ7.1.C635 Fi 2019 (print) | DDC [Fic]—dc23
LC record available at https://lccn.loc.gov/2018052677

Printed in the United States of America.
ISBN 9781984812506
1 3 5 7 9 10 8 6 4 2

Design by Ryan Thomann and Dave Kopka.
Text set in Chaparral.

To my husband and kids, who introduced me to camping
(with and without a dog),

and to the Van Ledtjkins, my other family

CHAPTER 1

Before we're even out the door, I know something has changed. For starters, Fetch Man is coming with us on our walk. He hasn't done that since we lived in the city. It's always just me and my short human, Hattie.

And that's not the only thing that's different. At the end of our driveway, instead of heading in the usual direction, we go the other way. Once we pass the house where my friends Goldie and Patches live, my nose picks up scents of humans and dogs I haven't met. And I never knew our neighborhood had so many cats!

My tail swishing, I pick up the pace. Maybe we're going to the real Dog Park, where lots of dogs come to play. Or to the pond where our whole family went for a delicious picnic when Nana was visiting. Yippee! Wherever it is, I'm SO ready!

I look back at Hattie as she runs her hand through what's left of her hair—add that to the list of changes. One day Hattie and Food Lady came home with shopping bags, and Hattie's bushy hair was gone!

Things are changing so fast these days, my guard is totally up. Fetch Man and Food Lady keep saying a word I used to hear when we lived in the city—"skool." I can't remember what it means. Every time they say this, Hattie's breathing speeds up and she smells worried. It's almost as if another change is coming and we're both afraid to find out what it is.

Changes have been happening outside, too. The plants in Food Lady's vegetable patch started drooping and sagging. Every now and then, a leaf flutters off the giant tree. Is it just a coincidence that I've seen more squirrels lately, too? I may be a professional, but there are a lot of them and only one of me! How am I supposed to keep my family safe?!

As we walk along, Hattie and Fetch Man's chatter is a curious mixture of business and excitement. Fetch Man pulls the slim box out of his pocket and taps it while he talks. Hattie nods a lot, walking faster than usual. Something is definitely up.

We turn at a noisy corner. At the next street, we turn again. More smells of humans and dogs I don't know. Different trees and fences, too. How big is our neighborhood anyway?

We pass a chubby man at the end of his driveway spraying a hose. A lady in sleek clothing waves hello as she runs by on the other side of the street. A boy whizzes past on a bike. I catch a whiff of grape jelly. And dirt. "Yahoo!" he shouts in a loud voice, a cloud of dust flying up behind him. Hattie turns her head and coughs.

Right when I think I'll never find out where we're headed, we stop at a grassy yard, where a white-haired man is clipping a hedge. He looks up and smiles, like a couple of humans and a handsome Jack Russell Terrier are exactly who he was expecting to see walk up his driveway.

He comes over and greets us, shaking Fetch Man's hand. His gait is relaxed and friendly, but a dog can never be too sure. My nose gets busy checking him out.

He squats down and scratches behind my ears. "Hey, pup," he says as I give him a lick.

Mmmmm! His hand tastes like a glazed doughnut. My tail thumps with approval.

Doughnut Man rises and gestures toward his open garage. "Here," he says.

As we follow him inside, Fetch Man's eyes bulge. His head swivels like he can't decide where to look. The garage is loaded with stuff stacked on shelves, hung on hooks, and piled in the back behind the pickup truck. "Wow!" he says, his voice full of admiration.

Sadly, the concrete floor is totally clean, as if no tasty wrappers or slobbery tennis balls have ever touched it. There are no toys, and no room to play, either.

What's so great about this place?

Doughnut Man grabs a long bag and carries it out to the grass in front of the house. As we gather around, he pulls out poles that bend and curve, flappy fabric with zippers, and a large mat. Fetch Man listens with rapt attention while Doughnut Man sets up the poles, chatting the whole time. He drapes the fabric on top, and it becomes a dome about the size of our car, with zipper doors and windows that look like the screens I'm not allowed to scratch at home. Talk about curious!

Even more curious, the whole thing reeks of pine trees and burnt marshmallows. And much more alarming—the strong and musky odors of wild animals! Hattie, who apparently can't smell these horrors, claps her hands and calls it a "tent."

I have a terrible feeling about this. "Watch out, Hattie!" I bark, leaping on her legs. "This thing is probably dangerous."

But she ignores me. The tall humans do, too. Doughnut Man ducks back into the garage and returns with an armful of what looks like great big umbrellas. Until he opens them up, and then they're chairs. Whoa! They smell just as horrifying as the tent.

Happy as can be, Fetch Man sinks down into the closest chair. Hattie plops into another. Her face is beaming, too.

Oblivious to my warnings, Fetch Man stands and gives Doughnut Man a bunch of papery strips from his pocket. Next thing I know, they've folded everything up and we're headed back down the driveway. Fetch Man carries the long bag. Two of the umbrella chairs are slung over his shoulder. Hattie's got one hanging from hers, too. Neither one seems concerned about how bad this stuff smells, or how loaded down they are. Actually, they seem kind of glad.

We go back the way we came, and just like that, the walk is over. After dropping everything in the garage, Hattie hauls me up to her room and closes the door. She starts opening drawers, pulling out shirts, shorts, and pants that smell brand-new, and gazing at them happily. Since when does Hattie care about clothes? And why are we inside when we could be outside playing?

I climb onto the bed and press my snout against the window screen. Something—or someone—is rustling in the leafy branches of the giant tree. A nasty squirrel clatters down the trunk, another one hot on his tail. My ears perk at horrific sounds.

Chipper, chatter, squawk!

Those squirrels are running wild in our Dog Park while I'm stuck in the house. "Come on, Hattie!" I bark. "Let's go outside!" I leap off the bed, romping at her heels. But all she does is dash around the room, ignoring me.

She tosses the clothes inside a big empty bag lying open on the floor. With each toss, she sighs, then takes the same clothes out again. She frowns at them like they're confusing. Or wrong. Didn't they make her happy a second ago? Finally, she opens the screen and thrusts her head and shoulders out the window.

I leap back onto the bed and poke my head outside, too. Sure enough, those two nasty squirrels are still chasing each other near the back fence. "Don't get any ideas, Rodents!" I bark. "I'm still in charge around here!"

Hattie scolds me, then calls, "Hey, Angel!" She cranes her head toward the house next door.

I gaze down into the Dog Park behind it. A Golden Retriever and a white dog with black patches are playing keep-away with a stick. My best friends, Goldie and Patches! They look extra energetic today. If only I weren't stuck inside . . .

F-f-f-f-t! A window flies up. Our friend Angel's head appears wearing a wide grin. "Hey!" she cries.

Hattie holds some of the clothes out the window, showing them to Angel. "Help! Help!" she calls.

Angel is clearly not interested. "No-big-deel," she says, frowning.

Whatever Angel said is not what Hattie wants to hear. With a huff, she whips the clothes back inside and lets them drop to the floor. She sticks her head back out the window. She asks Angel a bunch of questions. I hear her say "new-kid" a couple of times, sounding wavery. Nervous.

"It's okay." Angel's tone is reassuring. "No-big-deel," she keeps saying.

What's making Hattie so nervous? My ears perked, I listen my hardest, but Hattie and Angel aren't the only ones talking.

Chipper, chatter, squawk!

Down in our Dog Park, the two nasty squirrels continue scurrying around the tree, while another one digs a hole next to Food Lady's vegetable patch. Those squirrels are popping up everywhere!

My fur bristles. "I'm warning you!" I bark.

Hattie pushes me away—my cue to give up. "FEN-way," she scolds. She mutters some more at Angel, ending with "See-ya." She moves away from the window with another sigh. She smells disappointed, like Angel let her down somehow.

"Oh, Fenway," she says, collapsing on the bed. Clearly, she's as frustrated as I am.

I climb onto her lap. "Don't worry," I say, nuzzling into her shirt. "Your loyal dog is always here for you."

Hattie wraps her arms around me and kisses my brown paw, then my white paw. "Aw, Fenway." She reaches across me and tugs the bedside drawer open.

My tail wags with glee. Because I know what's coming next.

Hattie pulls out a familiar-looking notebook. "Shhh," she says, her finger to her lips. She flips to a blank page and begins sweeping a pencil across it.

Sswooosh-thsssss-thsssss . . . I watch as images appear. Soon there is a reptile with huge, powerful wings on the paper. And a girl with tiny delicate wings and short hair like Hattie's.

She makes more and more pictures. Lines and curves, too. "Comm-ix," she says, showing them to me. Each image is inside its own little box. Hattie flips through the pages, speaking in a soft yet energetic voice like she's telling me about an exciting day of romping in the Dog Park.

I lean into her shirt, sighing with happiness. My short human smells awfully proud. Our special comm-ix is one new thing that's actually pretty great.

Tap-tap-tap!

"Ready?" Fetch Man says. We both startle, and Hattie slams the book shut. She whips it behind her back as the door swings open and Fetch Man strides on through. His smiling face sags as his gaze lands on the empty bag.

Hattie shrugs and looks away.

"Bay-bee," he says, tussling her short hair. He sinks down next to us and speaks in an encouraging tone, like the first time we played ball with those fat, leathery gloves. I pick up a few words that I know: "new," "friends," and "play." But also a bunch that I don't: "fam-uh-lee," "camp-ing," and that mysterious word again—"skool."

When he finally stops talking, he pats her knee. "Okay?" he asks, getting up.

"Yeah," Hattie says, but she doesn't sound any better. When Fetch Man is gone, she drags the chair over to the closet. She takes a rolled-up blanket from the way-up-high shelf.

I rush over. It smells like pine trees and wild animals, like the umbrella chairs and the tent! Oh no!

I race around in circles, my mind in overdrive. "Skool" . . . the trip to Doughnut Man's garage . . . the bag and the rolled-up blanket . . . What does it all mean?

@HapteR 2

That night when the window gets dark, Hattie shuts it tight and climbs into bed. I cuddle up next to her. Good news: She smells like mint and vanilla like always. The other good news is I don't hear any suspicious sounds. My warnings must have scared those rodents away.

Somehow I manage to sleep, and I defeat even more nasty squirrels in my dreams. But when morning shines into the room, my suspicions go up again. Something big is about to change. I just know.

"Fenway," Hattie mumbles, rubbing her eyes. She smells as worried as I feel.

Good thing she's got a professional to keep her safe no matter what. "It's okay, Hattie," I bark. "I'll never let anything bad happen."

Hattie flings off the covers, apparently not reassured. She pulls on some clothes, then tugs them off with a loud sigh. After doing this more times than I can count, she's finally dressed.

"Don't worry—this day is going to be great!" I circle her legs, leaping and panting.

Hattie pats my back and heads into the Bathtub Room. I watch her make scrunched-up faces at the shiny square over the sink. "New-kid," she mutters to herself, pulling at her short hair.

I have to coax her down the stairs and into the Eating Place.

"Ready?" Food Lady asks.

"I'm so ready! I'm so ready!" I bark, rushing across the floor. Right away, I spy another change. Instead of standing at the counter or sitting at the table with steaming cups of coffee, Fetch Man and Food Lady are hard at work. Fetch Man's at the cabinet loading up a big bag with paper plates and cups and napkins, while Food Lady's bent over a plastic chest with wheels and a handle like a wagon. The Food Box!

My tail goes nuts! Is Food Lady packing sandwiches? Are we going on a picnic?

I race over to check it out. But before I'm even halfway there, my tongue starts dripping uncontrollably. I smell bacon and hot dogs! I leap up, my front paws gripping the top of the Food Box. Hey! This thing is stocked—eggs and milk and cheese and ketchup—

"FEN-way," Food Lady scolds, shooing me away.

My ears droop. What'd she expect? It's my job to know what food is coming on the picnic!

And speaking of jobs, the tall humans are in a huge hurry to do theirs. While Hattie eats a bowl of cereal, Fetch Man finishes packing the bag and starts on another. Food Lady puts ice on top of all the food. She shuts the Food Box and wheels it out to the garage.

"Hooray! Hooray! I love picnics!" I leap on Hattie's legs, and she goes over to grab my leash. She smells awfully nervous for somebody going on a picnic. I pull her through the front door.

As I'm mid-pee in the grass, I see something else that's different. The car is in the driveway instead of the garage. And it's got what looks like a big suitcase strapped on top!

Fetch Man shoves a bag into the back of the car. Whoa! It's totally stuffed!

Me and Hattie pile into the back seat. Food Lady lifts the Food Box in beside us. Then a bag that smells like outdoor toys. Soon we are so packed in, nothing else will fit.

The garage door bangs shut, and the car backs out of

the driveway. I climb onto Hattie's lap. When I stick my head out the window, I can't believe my eyes . . .

Another loaded-down car is backing out of the driveway next door. And my best friends' faces are staring back at me!

"'Sup, ladies?" I call, the breeze rippling my fur.

"We're going on a trip!" Patches calls.

My tail sags. "Oh no!" I bark. "I'll miss you so much."

"Don't be too sure!" Goldie yells back as the cars turn. Our car follows theirs as we zoom up the street.

We ride for a Long, Long Time. Finally, we are driving through a place that smells like pine and wild animals. And we're surrounded by tall trees. Are we in the woods?

I shudder. I'm not sure we belong here. Are we lost?

We cruise along slowly. The car jostles around curves and climbs up slopes. I sniff traces of smoke and burnt marshmallows.

Hattie's breathing quickens. She's worried again.

I'm about to reassure her that I've got this. But do I? Squirrels are bad enough. The woods are probably full of other wild animals. Can I handle them, too?

Soon the car pulls into a gravelly area and stops.

When it goes quiet, Fetch Man turns around and grins at Hattie. "Ready?" he says.

She smiles back and flings the door open. I'm right behind her.

As I tend to business in the pine needles, I sniff in every direction. We are in the woods, all right. Tall pine trees are everywhere. There are a few cars besides ours, each just as loaded down. Fetch Man and Food Lady head toward a building with a sharp, pointy roof. Its walls look like a bunch of trees stacked on top of each other. It even smells like wood.

As soon as me and Hattie romp through the door, I check the place out. We're in a huge open space. In front of me, glass cases are cold and full of ice. Shelves are lined with bottles and boxes and cans. T-shirts and lotions and stacks of wood, too. Is this a store?

On the far wall, I see a stone-covered fireplace that goes up to the ceiling. Comfy chairs sit on a rug that smells like millions of human feet. Are we in somebody's Lounging Room?

Fetch Man starts talking to a man behind a counter. He's unfolding a big sheet of paper and pointing. Food Lady peers over Fetch Man's shoulder and nods a lot. Whatever's on that paper must be awfully interesting. Even Hattie's staring at it.

Fetch Man folds the paper back up and goes over to the stacks of wood. Hattie lets me go, and as I scamper after him, my ears perk. Footsteps thud through the door. So do jingling dog tags.

"Hattie!" a familiar voice shouts.

I whip around as Angel rushes over with Tool Man and Muffin Lady. A Golden Retriever and a white dog with black patches trot up to us, their leashes dragging behind them. My tail goes nuts. "Ladies!" I bark. "I missed you so much!"

"Hey, Fenway," Patches calls, not sounding the least bit surprised to see me. Did she know I would be here in the woods?

"You just saw us this morning," Goldie says after we exchange bum-sniffs.

The humans don't seem surprised to see each other, either. They stand around chatting excitedly. Angel leads Hattie around the huge space, showing her everything like she's right at home. Has she been here before?

"I'm glad you didn't go away on that trip." I nuzzle Patches's fur. It would've been terrible if my best friends were really gone. "Did your humans decide to come on our picnic with us? We have tons of food. Trust me!"

Goldie cocks her head. *"Picnic?"*

16

"This is no picnic, Fenway," Patches says in her lovely voice. "We're going to live here."

"Not forever," Goldie corrects. "For three days."

"We do it every year at this time," Patches says.

Now I'm the one cocking my head. Did I hear them right? Do they realize we're in the woods? "But why?"

"It's tradition!" Patches announces proudly. "Just a few families at first, but once our sweet Angel started school, the group got bigger."

School. *Skool?* An image swirls in my mind. That place where short humans with backpacks went back in the city. But we never came to the woods. What are the ladies talking about? Are there two different schools? Is Hattie going to this other school?

No wonder she's been worried. She must've known about this whole woods and wild animals tradition. Talk about something worth worrying about!

"Precious Angel loves to be with her school friends," Patches says. "They call themselves 'the crew.'"

"Well, some of them act like friends," Goldie grumbles. "And some of them don't."

Patches shoots her a scolding look. "Now, Goldie . . ."

"Um, ladies, did you say we're going to live here?" I glance around the big space. "Me and my humans can curl up on the comfy furniture, but what about everybody else?"

"Not in *here*," Goldie says. "Outside!"

My fur stands on end. "With the trees? And the wild—woods?"

"Relax, Fenway. It'll be fun," Patches says, nosing my neck. "Picture families and dogs romping around, being together. Making new friends. Doesn't that sound great?"

"It sure does." My hopes soar. "Yippee! I love making new friends!"

"We noticed," Goldie mutters.

"Most everyone's friendly," Patches says. "You'll be a big hit."

"Hopefully," Goldie says, her snout scrunching. "Let's not forget what happened last year."

I shrink back. "What are you ladies talking about?"

"Oh, don't worry. Just some troublemakers," Patches explains. "I'm sure everything will be fine this time."

If the ladies slept outside in the woods for three whole nights, it's no shock that troublemakers showed up. Obviously, that means wild animals, and Goldie and Patches were caught off guard. They are not professionals.

But now they have me.

CHaPteR 3

Then something very confusing happens.
Just when I thought we were going to stay here—isn't
that what the ladies said?—we pile back in the cars. Did
the humans suddenly smell the wild animals and decide to head back home?

Maybe not. Instead of turning toward the paved
road, we travel deeper into the woods. And instead of
zooming, the car seems to be creeping. Food Lady un-
folds the big sheet of paper and appears to be studying
it. I stick my head out the window, but there's barely
enough breeze to blow my ears back. The woods are

alive with tantalizing scents—pancakes and bacon. My tongue drips with excitement.

They're alive with sounds, too. I don't hear any wild animals except some birds singing. Humans are chattering and shouting, too. I get the birds, but how many humans are in these woods, anyway?

"Here," Food Lady says, pointing out the window.

The car makes a turn, and we bump along into a clearing. The human sounds are louder. We pass stopped cars and tents like ours except they're boxy or pointy instead of rounded. Beside each tent is a wooden table with benches like the ones at the pond or the park. Humans are busy unloading cars. And there's something else I see . . .

Dogs!

My tail starts wagging. A small dog races around in circles, clutching a Frisbee. A Chocolate Lab with a bandanna lopes after her. Wowee, dogs are playing keep-away in the woods! How can I get in on the action?

When the road ends, the car pulls onto the grass and shudders to a stop. I leap out of the car, and my tail goes wild again. Because up ahead near a big oak tree, the ladies are bounding out of their car! I don't know why we are all stopping at this clearing, but it sure seems like a good idea. I can hardly wait to play!

I start to romp over to my friends when a yank on the leash pulls me back. "Fenway!" Hattie cries.

We halt in the matted-down dirt in front of an empty wooden table. Behind it, I smell ashes and . . . *sniff, sniff* . . . the lingering aroma of hot dogs?

I bounce, my tongue ready to drip. Hot dogs?! I love hot dogs!

Hattie hangs back while Food Lady and Fetch Man shake hands with other tall humans. She shifts her weight like she's uncomfortable. Or bashful.

Up ahead, I see a short human with dark curly hair waving at us. It's Angel! Hattie must spy her at the exact same time, because we hurry toward her and the ladies under the big oak tree.

My tail sways happily. "Yippee!" I say to them. "Now that we're back together, let's play! That Frisbee chase looks like fun."

As the short humans chat, Goldie scowls in the direction of the other dogs. "Plenty of time for that," she says.

"What do you mean?" I say, looking around. "I'm so excited to make new friends, like you said. And some of them are already having fun without us."

Patches looks like she's thinking for a second. "Yes, but we don't want to get off on the wrong paw."

21

"Let's just relax for a bit," Goldie says.

The ladies sure picked a bad time to finally agree on something. Well, if they don't want to play, I know somebody who does. I leap on Hattie's legs, giving her that face she can't resist. "We were in the car for such a Long, Long Time!" I bark. "How about a game of fetch?"

"Aw, Fenway." She pats my head, but she's looking at Fetch Man. He's unloading the big case on top of the car.

"Hattie," he calls.

Hattie leads me to the wooden table, then stoops down like she's tying her sneaker. She rushes up to take a bag from Fetch Man.

I go to follow, but—hey! My leash is tangled around the table leg. "Bad news, everybody!" I bark. "I'm stuck!"

All around us, humans are focused and busy. A boxy tent rises up near the spot where we saw Angel and the ladies. Goldie and Patches are lying in the shade of the big oak tree like they have nothing else to do. The two romping dogs from before are nowhere in sight.

Vwoop! Fetch Man unzips the long bag and hands Hattie pole after pole. Food Lady spreads out a large plastic mat as Fetch Man hammers metal stakes in the dirt, then takes them out as if he can't decide where they should go. The humans' faces are puzzled, and they're chattering all at once—and not noticing me.

"Um, hello!" I bark, lunging as far as I can. "I can't reach you guys, and it's really boring over here!"

"FEN-way," Fetch Man grumbles, barely looking up from hammering the last stake. He's not making one move to come over here and set me free. Food Lady, either. She's turning some big, floppy fabric one way, then another, then around and around, while Hattie starts handing Fetch Man the curved poles. Fetch Man sighs like he's frustrated.

I sure know the feeling. "Guys, I'm serious!" I bark even louder. "I can't get away from this table leg. My leash got wrapped around it somehow!"

Fetch Man shoots an annoyed look in my direction. Food Lady, too. Then they both turn to Hattie.

At last, my hard work pays off. Hattie hurries over, and just like that, I'm free. Well, I'm still on the leash, but at least I'm not stuck to the table leg.

We stroll past the ladies' car. Tool Man and Muffin Lady are stuffing rolled-up blankets and pillows into the boxy tent. "Angel?" Hattie asks.

Angel emerges from the tent, her eyes full and excited. Next thing I know, she's grabbed the ladies' leashes. Hooray! We're going for a walk! I'm so excited!

But as Angel leads us toward a path in the woods, my hackles shoot up. Because the woods are loaded with suspicious signs.

Pine trees line the trail like tall, tall fences. When I look up, all I see are treetops. Where did the sky go? Is it still up there?

There's hardly any light, except for small bright spots on the ground. It's noisy, too, with chirps and trills and buzzes I've never heard before. And scents of wood and leaves and pests like squirrels and chipmunks. Plus strange animals that smell even worse than bunnies. My paw just misses stepping on a tail that slithers away through the brush. At least I think it was a tail?

The ladies' ears flap back against their heads like they're not concerned. Don't they notice how scary the woods are?

By the time I decide to ask them, I pick up different, stronger sounds and scents—humans. And dogs! Lots of dogs!

The path ends, and we cross a road. Whew! We're finally out of the woods. Ahead of us is a huge clearing. In the distance, I spy a small house and a pond. And right in front of us is a big maple tree and a grassy area with a chain-link fence around it. It smells fantastic, and it sounds even better! I know what this is!

"Wowee!" I bark, jumping and spinning. "It's a Dog Park!"

"Now, remember what we said," Goldie mutters. The

short humans steer us to the gate, where it's cool and shady.

I'm leaping on it before Angel can get it open. "You said something?"

"Fenway—" Patches starts to say as I burst inside. Whatever she wants to tell me can wait until later.

Because my leash is unhooked, and I'm free! I zoom by a dark-haired short human on a bench near the giant water dish. I tear around the Dog Park, passing a climbing ramp, a crawling tube, and, best of all, frolicking dogs! As I make a wide arc and come around the other way, I realize the small dog clutching a Frisbee and the Chocolate Lab with a bandanna are probably the same two I saw earlier.

Hattie and Angel linger near the gate. I spy Goldie and Patches chasing each other off to the side, not joining in the game. They must not know how things work at the Dog Park. I guess they have a lot to learn.

Slowing, I prance up to the new dogs.

"Fenway!" I hear Patches call.

Clearly, the ladies want me to play with them. But we can do that any old time.

"'Sup, guys?" I say, and the new dogs whip their heads around. "I'm Fenway. Do you come here a lot?"

The small dog drops the Frisbee. She gives me a

once-over, then wanders up to smell my bum. After the Quickest Sniff Ever, she turns away before I can return the greeting. What's up with that? Could she possibly make up her mind about me that fast?

I check her out as best I can. Smells like a Pomeranian. She's almost my size, but her fur is tan-colored. And it's so puffed out, she's practically round. The other dog hangs back, his tail sagging. I can't tell if he's shy or lazy.

"Fenway, huh?" she says cautiously, her black eyes and nose popping out from all that fur. "I don't remember you from last year. Or any other year."

I drop onto my forepaws. "Newsflash! I'm here now!" I snatch the Frisbee and take off.

"Hey!" she calls from behind me.

Ha! Now the fun can begin! I run halfway around the Dog Park before I realize she's not following me. Nobody is. I gaze back toward the front of the park. The Pomeranian is standing her ground, yawning. The Chocolate Lab is sunk down into the grass, halfheartedly licking a paw.

Maybe they're tired. I trot over to the ladies, who have stopped chasing each other and are now just snapping at flies. I let the Frisbee fall. "Wanna play?"

The ladies exchange an uncomfortable look.

"What?"

Patches glances over at the Pomeranian, who's in the exact same spot, her fur raised in anger. Though she's so fluffy, it's kind of hard to tell. "I'm afraid you stepped on Coco's paws," she says in her lovely voice.

"I did not!" I say. "The only thing my paws stepped on was grass."

"It's an expression," Goldie gruffs. "Coco's the boss. If you don't do things her way, your name is mud."

"My name is—"

"That's an expression, too," Goldie cuts in.

Patches looks pained. "It means she won't like you."

My ears droop, and I take a step back. "I was just trying to be friendly."

Patches comes up and noses my neck. "We know."

"And you took her Frisbee," Goldie says. She plucks it from the grass and lopes over to the Pomeranian—Coco—who turns away like she's lost interest.

"Seriously?" I say, gazing at Coco sideways. "What's her deal?"

Patches starts to say something, but right then a branch creaks. Leaves rustle. And Hattie lets out a hair-raising shriek.

Chapter 4

A boy plops out of the sky and lands inside the Dog Park right in front of Hattie and Angel. "Yahoo!" he yells, laughing. He smells like grape jelly. And dirt.

I didn't hear the gate open. How did this boy get into the Dog Park? And why is his scent so familiar?

Angel grimaces at the boy, her arms folded. "MAR-cus," she says. Her voice sounds scolding.

Before heading over to check him out, I gaze at Hattie. She's gasping like she's trying to catch her breath, her face pale. She's clearly anxious. She glances up at the big maple tree, where a fat branch is hanging over the Dog Park fence.

The boy keeps on laughing. When he comes up for air, he squints at Hattie. "Hey," he says. "Yoo-new?"

Breathing quickly, Hattie forces a smile. "Hattie," she says in a low voice. Even from here, I can smell how nervous she is. Clearly, she needs her loyal dog. I pivot and sprint toward her.

"Don't worry, Hattie!" I nuzzle her leg. "I'm here now!"

"Scared-ya!" Marcus says, laughing again.

"Nuh-uh," she says, rubbing my head a couple of times. Suddenly, she springs up like she just got an idea.

As Angel keeps speaking to Marcus in that scolding voice, Hattie rushes out of the gate. Before I can even wonder if she's abandoning me, she grabs onto a low branch and skitters up the trunk of the big maple tree.

I scamper to the fence and leap up, my claws clutching the chain links of the fence. "Hattie, what are you doing?"

When she reaches the fat branch that hangs over the Dog Park, she crawls out into the rustling leaves. She crouches low as if she's hiding. But we can all see her.

Marcus gazes up, a huge smile on his face. "Jump!" he yells.

"Don't!" Angel shouts at the same time.

But Hattie's already let go of the branch. She free-falls into the Dog Park and lands—*plop!*—one knee up and one smacking the ground.

"Ta-da!" she cries, springing up. She's wearing a grin, but that doesn't always mean she's happy.

I rush over to make sure she smells all right.

"Same old Marcus," I hear Goldie grumble under her breath.

"Give him a chance," Patches murmurs. "Maybe he's changed."

"Sure doesn't look like it," Goldie growls.

"Sweet!" Marcus cries, striding up to Hattie with his arm outstretched. At first, I think he's going to hug her, but instead he slaps her hand. "The crew!"

"The crew!" Hattie says, slapping him back. Since when does she do that? Is this a new kind of short human greeting? Maybe Hattie isn't sure, either. Her face flushes and she looks away. She rubs her dirty knee, wincing. Is this boy bothering her?

He's sure bothering me. I romp over and jump on his legs, my nose hard at work. He doesn't smell nearly as friendly as a short human should. Besides dirt and jelly and that maple tree, he smells confident. Too confident.

"Hey!" Marcus yells, his arm shooing. "Get lost!"

My ears sag and I back away. I was only checking him out. How else am I supposed to know if he's threatening?

Hattie rushes between me and Marcus. She grabs my collar, her shoulders slumping like she feels bad.

"Sorry," she says. I think she's talking to me for a second, but then I notice she's looking at him.

I glance up at her. "Why are you taking his side?" I whine.

Hattie scowls. "Shhh!"

"Keep your nose on that mutt," a dog's voice says with disgust. When I turn, I see Coco and that Chocolate Lab with the bandanna. The Frisbee that Goldie returned to her is lying in the grass, untouched. "I don't trust him."

It's pretty clear she's talking about me, but why? I'm still trying to figure her out when the sounds of squealing short humans and jingling dog tags capture everybody's attention. We turn as all kinds of short humans race into the Dog Park with a pack of dogs.

"Coco!" the dogs call in unison. They head straight for the Pomeranian, their tails wagging happily, like they can't wait to greet an old friend.

She stands tall in all her poofy-ness, her head turned as if she doesn't even notice the new dogs rushing toward her. What she lacks in excitement, the Chocolate Lab more than makes up for. He's leaping and running in circles, like it's the greatest day of his life. "Ohmygosh! Ohmygosh!" he keeps yapping.

"Marcus!" some of the short humans yell, surrounding him. One of them bumps his fist. Another slaps him on the back. A couple smack hands with Angel. "The crew," I hear them say. Either they don't see Hattie standing there, too, or they are totally ignoring her.

Marcus must notice because he waves Hattie into the group. All of a sudden, everyone's smiling and talking. Somebody claps Hattie on the shoulder. "The crew," some of them say.

I turn to the ladies. "What's so special about that boy Marcus? Is he in charge of the treats or something?"

Goldie sneers. "He has some kind of special power over everyone. Even you backed away when he told you to."

My tail droops. She has a point there.

"Funny, but the only one who doesn't pay attention to him is his own dog," Patches says.

I cock my head. "But he came out of the tree. He didn't have a dog with him," I say.

"That's because she was already here." Goldie glances toward the center of the Dog Park and nods.

I turn to see which dog she's looking at, my ears picking up the sounds of clinking tags and yipping dogs. Coco struts slowly across the grass, her snout in the air. A pack of dogs trails behind: a three-legged German Shepherd, a huge black Poodle, and a Dachshund panting with excitement. Their tails are swinging eagerly, even though Coco's not racing or playing keep-away or doing anything fun. The bandanna-wearing Chocolate Lab drops back for a quick scratch, then hurries to re-join the others as if he's afraid he might miss the party. Don't those dogs realize we're in a huge Dog Park with a climbing ramp and a crawling tube, not to mention a Frisbee? Then I remember what Goldie said about who's the boss.

"Wait—Marcus's dog is *Coco*?" I ask.

I watch Coco wander over to the back fence and curl up in the shade. The other dogs look at each other for a second. Then they drop down, too, as if they can't think of anything better to do than relax. Or maybe they're lost without Coco leading the way.

"Like canine, like human," Goldie grumbles.

I turn toward the front of the Dog Park. The new short humans are still swarmed around Marcus. I guess he does have special powers, because they stare at him like he's a plate of juicy steaks. "Marcus and Coco really are a lot alike," I say to the ladies.

Just then, Marcus shouts, "Go!" and takes off. The others race after him through the grass, whooping and hollering. Hattie and Angel seem all too glad to join in.

My tail goes nuts. Wowee! It's a game of chase! I bolt toward them. "Hey, everybody!" I bark. "Wait for me!"

Marcus leaps up and over the climbing ramp, the

other short humans following his every move. They may be fast, but they clearly have no strategy. They'll never catch him unless they try to head him off.

Luckily, when it comes to playing chase, I'm a professional! I make a wide arc and race around to the crawling tube from the far side. I shoot through one end just as Marcus's head appears in the other.

"Gotcha!" I bark, scampering toward him. I'm going to win!

But when I'm only midway through the tube, his eyes widen like he's surprised. Or scared. Suddenly, he ducks back out.

I should've known it wouldn't be that easy. I race through the crawling tube and burst out after him. I spy him tearing through the grass at high speed, his arms flailing. And laughing hysterically. "Help! Help!" he cries in a voice that doesn't sound the least bit afraid.

The other short humans laugh, too. Some of them make frightened faces and rush away from me, shouting and giggling as I approach. They're looking and acting totally panicked, in spite of the laughing. But none of them smells scared at all. Even Hattie is going along with this new part of the game. Why is Hattie acting panicked? It's just little old me!

I chase the short humans from one end of the Dog Park to the other. I can't help but notice that none of the other dogs are joining in. "Hey, come on, everybody!" I yell as I pass by. "Don't you want to join this really fun game of chase?"

Some of the dogs start panting. Tails wag, too. But nobody's making a move. The whole pack turns to Coco, who stares back at them, sitting perfectly still. Sure, the ladies said she's the boss. But Dog Parks are for playing. She was pretty into that Frisbee before.

Hey! Maybe she just needs an especially friendly dog to entice her to play with it again. I make a sharp turn and zip over to the Frisbee—*chomp!* I sprint up to Coco, dropping it right at her paws. "I've got a great idea!" I cry. "We can all play Frisbee. And I'll let you have it first!" I gaze at her excitedly, my tail thumping. She can't possibly resist!

At first, Coco just glares at me. She doesn't even get up. Then she cocks her head questioningly, like she's not sure she heard me right. "Wow," she says, not sounding excited at all. "Thanks for *letting* me be the first to be chased. With my own Frisbee."

My tail slows its thumps. Coco's tone tells me something's wrong. But what? She obviously loves playing Frisbee. "Hey, guys," I say, slinking over to the other dogs. "Don't you want to play?" The only one who bounds right up and gives me a welcoming sniff is the bandanna-wearing Chocolate Lab.

"Ohmygosh! Ohmygosh!" he says, slobbering all over me. He tells me his name is Lucky. He smells like he's itching to play.

I move on to give the Dachshund a friendly sniff before reaching up to smell the German Shepherd and the huge black Poodle. They're both way bigger than the rest of us, even Goldie. And they're still as statues. Instead of wagging their tails or greeting me back, they gaze cautiously at Coco. Lucky nods toward each of the other dogs, telling me their names are Chorizo, Titan, and Midnight.

"Dude!" I say, turning to the Dachshund. "Your name is Chorizo? I LOVE chorizo!"

The Dachshund perks up. "Thanks. I get that a lot. Apparently, my humans think I look like a sausage."

I tilt my head. "They do?"

"Um, I think we'll figure out our own game, thank you very much," Coco sneers, nosing her way between us and shaking out her extra-fluffy fur. "*Fenway*, is it?" She says my name like it tastes horrible. Like a fruity peach. Or blueberries. *Blech!* Next thing I know, her snout is back in the air and the rest of the dogs are following her toward the front of the Dog Park.

The ladies trot up to me. "What just happened?" I ask.

"You've got a lot to learn," Goldie says.

Patches nuzzles my ruff. "Be patient, Fenway. You'll get used to her."

I look across the grass at the other dogs. I'm about to ask if I have to get used to the rest of them, too, but then I notice the short humans grabbing leashes. Is it time to go already? We haven't had any fun yet!

"Fenway!" Hattie calls, holding my leash. For some reason, she sounds just as anxious to leave as everybody else.

Marcus opens his hand, and the Frisbee flies into it. "Cool!" shouts the cap-wearing boy who's standing right where the Frisbee used to be. Coco, her sparkly collar gleaming through her poofy fur, leads Marcus through the gate, her snout still in the air.

As me and Hattie wait for Angel to clip the ladies' leashes, I notice the short human on the bench near the giant water dish. A long, dark braid hangs over her shoulder and there's white paint on her cheek that looks kind of like a horse. Her eyes are focused on a book in her lap. Has she not looked up the whole time we've been here? Lucky saunters over, the end of his bandanna flapping in the breeze.

"Who's she?" I say to the ladies.

"June?" Goldie asks. "She used to be part of the crew, but it doesn't look like it anymore."

"That must be why she's sitting all by herself," Patches says.

I gaze at her, my head cocked. "That makes no sense. Short humans love to play with other short humans. Like dogs!"

"Most do," Patches says. "But not all."

CHapteR 5

Me and Hattie traipse back through the woods with Angel and the ladies, my hackles up the whole time. I spy a rotting tree trunk lying on top of the feathery ground plants. Who could knock *that* over? The end facing us is jagged, like it was gnawed by a huge mouth. I shudder. A pair of chittering chipmunks chases each other up and over the raggedy bark. I shudder some more.

The path is thick with smells—damp soil, pine needles, rodent-y pests, and that strong, musky odor I picked up before. The more I try to ignore it, the more it wafts into my nose. Are scary creatures hiding underground? Behind the rocks? Way up in the trees?

I'm thinking so hard I can barely keep up with the pack. Those mysterious wild animals will probably strike when we least expect it. "Don't get any funny ideas!" I bark, trying to sound fiercer than I feel. "Mess with us and you'll be sorry!"

"Fenway, shhh," Hattie says over her shoulder.

Why isn't she letting me do my job? I shut my mouth, but I keep my eyes peeled. Fortunately, I don't see anything more dangerous than a fat tree root the rest of the way.

As we get to the little clearing where we were before, my nostrils pulse with the scent of burning wood. Smoke, too. And where there's smoke, there's usually—

"FIRE!" I bark, jumping up and pulling on the leash. "Look out, everybody! This place is on fire!"

The ladies are not alarmed at all. They keep on walking toward the smoky smell. So do the short humans.

What's wrong with everybody? Good thing I'm here! "Run for your lives!" I bark. "We're in terrible danger!"

"Fenway, heel!" Hattie scolds, pulling me back. She's headed right for the fire! I can hear it popping and crackling. Flames and dark smoke are rising up from the ground. Doesn't she see it?

"Hattie, watch out!" I bark.

But she doesn't even react. "See-ya," she says as Angel and the ladies veer off at the big oak tree. *Vwoop!* An opening appears in the boxy tent, and I watch them disappear inside.

As Hattie leads me toward the wooden table near the dirt road and our car, I spy Fetch Man crouching on the ground behind a burning pile of wood surrounded by rocks. He's poking the fire with some kind of tool. I tell myself to calm down. I have a feeling it's a grill, even though it doesn't look anything like the one we have at home. Fetch Man seems to have it under control. For now.

As we approach the table, I do a double take. A domed tent has popped up. Chairs, too. And that's not all. If my eyes aren't mistaken, right next to the table is a long box with a white lid. It has handles on the sides and wheels on the bottom. It can only be one thing— our Food Box!

I leap and twirl. "Hooray! Hooray!" I bark, my tummy rumbling. "I knew we were going to have a picnic!"

Hattie marches up to Food Lady, who's at the table chopping vegetables like she does in the Eating Place at home. "Yum!" Hattie says, sliding onto a bench. She grabs a piece of cucumber and crunches a bite.

"What about me? I love picnics!" I bark, trying to leap onto her lap. Even though that cucumber smells bland and tasteless, there's bound to be something delicious up there, like a pretzel or a slice of cheese.

"Off!" Hattie snaps.

"Hey, dogs like snacks, too!" I bark as I slink away,

and—what? Somehow my leash got tied around the leg of the bench again. I tug and tug, but I'm totally stuck.

"Fenway, stay," Hattie commands, then goes back to chattering with Food Lady.

I sink into the matted-down dirt. We left the Dog Park for this? Lying under the table alone with nothing to eat? I sigh into my brown paw, covering my snout with the white one. I look out at the clearing.

It's dotted with humans and tents and smoke. On the opposite side of the dirt road sits another car and a boxy tent. Directly across the clearing, there's a pointy tent, a tall pine tree, and a hammock with a man sitting up and waving. "Hello!" Hammock Man calls. He looks awfully friendly. Hattie waves back.

I check out the rest of the area. The big oak tree and the path from the Dog Park are on our other side, along with that boxy tent that Angel and the ladies disappeared inside.

The place is alive with noise and activity. Fetch Man's not the only tall human hovering near fire and smoke. Everyone else is at tables working or hanging around holding plastic cups and chatting.

I feel myself dozing for a moment. Or maybe longer. Because when my eyes pop open, I can hardly believe my nose. Wowee! Are those—*slurp!*—smoky, salty hot dogs I smell?

Whoopee! I leap to my paws, my tail swishing with excitement. *Sniff . . . sniff . . .* My nose takes in loads of smoky scents—fish, peppers, baked beans, and that best scent of all, hot dogs!!!

Hattie grabs my leash. "Let's go, Fenway," she says, as if I need to be told to romp toward those yummy aromas. Apparently, the tall humans have the same idea because they come along, too. Food Lady's carrying a bowl of salad while Fetch Man brings a platter of fish.

Crossing the dirt road, we approach a wooden table with a boy sitting on top, his hand inside a crinkly bag. A lady whose arm is covered with swirly designs waggles a finger at him, her face scowling. The boy shrugs and slithers onto the bench, stuffing a handful of chips in his mouth. He smells familiar, like grape jelly. And dirt. Marcus!

Food Lady speaks to Swirly-Arm Lady. She takes noisy foil off a dish that smells like baked beans.

Sniff . . . sniff . . . Those hot dogs are sizzling on another Fire Space in the ground behind the table. My tongue drips with desire. My tail twirls in circles. I strain against the leash. "Let me at those hot dogs!" I bark.

Hattie's hand taps my head. "Fenway, shhh!"

Only Fetch Man seems to have the right idea. After setting the fish on the table, he strides over to the Fire

Space, where a broad-shouldered man is squatted down and prodding those glorious hot dogs. I go to follow, but Hattie drags me up to the bench where Marcus is sitting.

That mouthwatering scent is driving me nuts! "Please, Hattie!" I whine, trying to pull her toward the Fire Space. "What are we waiting for? Aren't you hungry?"

Totally ignoring me—and the hot dogs—Hattie slaps Marcus's outstretched palm. I'm suddenly aware that he and the tall humans are glancing at me with curious eyes. Like they're surprised someone noticed they were barbecuing hot dogs.

My ears pick up the sounds of jingling dog tags. Apparently, other dogs have noticed, too. I turn and see the ladies leading Angel right toward us. Beside them, Muffin Lady carries a tray that smells like spicy peppers and onions. Long, metal tongs swing from her belt. Tool Man's basket smells like warm tortillas.

And they're not the only ones headed this way. Across the clearing, Lucky, the Chocolate Lab, tows a slender man with pulled-back hair and shiny rings on his ears. I recognize him right away as the friendly Hammock Man. A lady with a big, round belly waddles next to him, her arms wrapped around a bowl heaped with steaming cobs of corn. Behind them trails a short human clutching a book against her chest. It's June! The one who was sitting alone at the Dog Park.

I remember the ladies said not all short humans like to play with each other. I wonder why.

I cock my head, watching June. She looks like a regular short human to me. Except maybe for the shuffling gait and slouching shoulders. And the way she's clenching that book like it's the most important thing in the world. Her body language is saying she's on the outside of the pack.

"Fenway!" the ladies cry. Suddenly, we're free from our leashes, exchanging bum sniffs.

Lucky joins in, too. "Ohmygosh! Ohmygosh!" he yaps. He smells as excited as I feel.

"Good thing you all showed up!" I say. "We're going to have a picnic!"

"Are you sure about that?" Goldie says, nodding at the humans who are gathering around the table without us.

Well, not for long! I bound over to the table where the hot dogs sit glistening on a paper plate. I leap up and up, my nose going nuts. "Let me at 'em!" I bark.

"Fenway, down!" Hattie scolds, as rustling sounds come from behind us.

I shiver. I don't smell a wild animal, but my nose tells me to be cautious, anyway. When I turn around, I'm snout to snout with . . .

"Coco?" I say, taking a step back. "Where did you come from?"

She responds with a glare, her sparkly collar glinting in the evening sun. The flaps of the boxy tent make a frame around her body. Inside, front and center, I spot a plush dog bed with lots of frills. I guess I have my answer.

"Why were you in there when the food is out here?"

The Pomeranian growls. "Trust me, Fenway, I have better things to do."

"What could be better than a picnic?"

"Give her some space," Patches says, gently nosing me away. We watch Coco give herself a shake, her fur poofing out more than ever.

Lucky sniffs the air. "Ohmygosh! Ohmygosh—hot dogs!"

"Finally, somebody has the right idea," I say, nosing his side. "Let's go beg for scraps!"

"Um, I don't think so." Coco's tone stops me in my tracks. I watch her strut over to a woolen blanket in front of a big metal bin that smells like garbage. "I'll decide when it's time to eat," she mutters, sinking onto the blanket.

Lucky looks at Coco, then back at me and the ladies. "I guess we should just hang out," he says, excitement visibly draining from him. He saunters to the blanket and flops down at the edge.

"All right, let's join the others," Patches murmurs.

Before I can open my mouth to argue, she and Goldie are already on their way to the blanket. They lie down with the other dogs, away from the table. And the yummy food.

Huh? Because Coco likes waiting, suddenly we all do? Well, not me! I hate waiting!

I scamper around the table, sizing things up. The humans are crowded up and down both sides, tall humans at one end, the short ones at the other. They're all totally busy chatting and munching. Or *almost* all.

June seems more interested in the open book on her lap than Hattie beside her. Or the food on her plate. I park myself at Hattie's sneakers, just like at home. As she takes a bite of food, I gaze up eagerly. Sooner or later, tasty crumbs or a yummy drip will fall. I slurp my chops.

Across from Hattie, Marcus is speaking nonstop. Every now and then, I hear Angel say, "Uh-huh."

Hattie turns to June. "Cool-yoon-ih-corn," she says, focusing on June's white-smudged cheek. It really does look like a horse.

49

"Thanks," June murmurs without looking up.

Marcus kicks Angel under the table, and I hear him snicker. Hattie smells uncomfortable. June does, too. For the rest of suppertime, June's eyes stay fixed on that book in her lap, while Hattie's are on her plate.

When the tall humans begin clearing the table or heading to the garbage bin, Marcus grabs a bag of marshmallows. "June-ih-corn!" he snickers, as the short humans—except for June—follow him to the Fire Space. At first, I wonder if I should warn Hattie about the fire, but one sniff tells me it's nearly died out. And besides, I smell a higher priority right here.

Swirly-Arm Lady heads over to a Food Box carrying a flimsy paper plate, one hot dog rolling back and forth with her every step. This can only mean one thing: opportunity!

I leap on her legs, my tongue panting and drooling.

"What the—?" she says, glancing down, just as . . .

Plop! The hot dog lands on the ground. I'm on it in a flash. *CHOMP! Mmmmm!* My mouth explodes with the juicy, spicy flavors. And a bit of dirt, too. I chomp and chomp, lost in magical wonder until, sadly, the wonderful hot dog is gone.

I feel Swirly-Arm Lady pat my head. And when I gaze up, she's laughing. "Smart-boy!"

Clearly, she wanted to share all along. But apparently

not everyone approves of my tactics. Coco scuttles over from the blanket, her ears and tail high. "That hot dog was mine!" she shouts at me.

I shirk away. "Weren't you watching? She dropped it. It was up for grabs!"

"She was bringing it to me." Her nose in the air, she whirls around in all her poofy-ness. As I watch her strut back to the blanket, I have a feeling what I did is going to come back and bite me.

Chapter 6

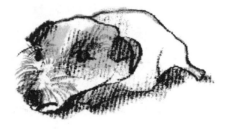

Way after the kibble's eaten and the sky
goes dark, Hattie carries me inside our tent. We curl up
together, zipped between a couple of padded blankets.
She gives each of my paws a quick kiss, then nuzzles
my neck. No notebook of comm-ix. No fur brushing. No
singing "best buddies."

Instead, she whispers at me for a Long, Long Time.
She mutters that upsetting word, "new-kid," again.
Clearly, she is afraid of something—maybe the wild
animals. They're mere pawsteps away!

I snuggle against her cheek. She has to know that
I'm always here to protect her.

"Aw, Fenway," she replies with a yawn.

My mouth opens for my own big yawn, even though I'm not the least bit sleepy. I give my head a vigorous shake and try to settle down. Crickets are chirping. Owls are hooting. And rustling sounds drift in from the forest. My fur prickles. Wild animals are outside, roaming free. I have to stay on guard.

A moment later, Hattie's asleep, her breathing calm and peaceful. Good thing she feels safe and protected with her ferocious dog at her side. But there's only so much I can do from inside this tent. My ears and nose will have to work overtime!

My jaws stretch open for another yawn. I've never been more alert. Nothing can distract me from protecting Hattie. Not even my droopy eyelids. Not even my heavy, heavy eyelids.

I let them flutter shut—just for a second. I hear Food Lady and Fetch Man crawling in and settling down on the other side of the tent.

I feel my body relax. And suddenly, I'm not in the tent with my humans anymore. I'm tramping through the dark, noisy forest, my body tingling with bravery. I have a job to do. I have to keep Hattie safe.

But it's so dark, I can't see anything. Good thing I can smell. And hear. Though I almost wish I couldn't.

Because the smells are alarming, like smoke and creatures I can't identify. Lots and lots of them. Some smell like birds. Some smell like rodents. But others smell strange, mysterious. Like grape jelly. And dirt.

Way up high, branches rustle and crack. Peeps and squeals echo through the woods. Throaty hooting, too: The-crew! The-crew!

Yikes! That voice sounds awfully menacing. "Go away!" I whimper, my tail wilting. I crawl under the pine needles, which feel strangely like Hattie's pillow. And smell oddly like mint and vanilla.

"Fenway?" Hattie's soft voice mumbles.

"Hattie?" I bark, turning toward her sleepy face. "What are you doing here in the scary woods?"

Instead of answering, she runs her hand through her short hair. She reaches for her backpack, pulling out shirts and shorts and socks and jackets, one after another after another. She strokes each one like it's a treasured friend, even though they smell brand-new and never worn before. Why is she interested in clothes at a time like this?

"Hattie," I bark. "This forest is full of danger. We have to scram. Like, RIGHT NOW!"

But she doesn't understand the huge problem. Now she's focused on a group of short humans. Where did they come from?

I recognize Angel and that loud boy Marcus. "The-crew!

The-crew!" they chant. Other short humans—boys and girls of different sizes—swoop in and join the chanting.

Hattie laughs. "The-crew! The-crew!" She slaps their palms.

The short humans zip around a tree, hop over a rock, and—

Oh no! Hattie's rushing straight toward an open mouth with giant fangs ready to chomp!

I shake with courage. There's no time to lose! It's up to me to save her. I have to make her listen. "Hattie, stop! Please!" I bark. "Or this will end in disaster!"

Hattie keeps going. She must not hear me. I race as fast as I can, trying to head her off, before she—

THUD! Crash!

My eyes pop open. Dim morning light seeps into the tent. I climb out from the zipped-up blanket and give myself a good stretch.

"Fenway," Hattie murmurs, patting my head.

"I'm so happy to see you!" I bark, romping up to her pillow. I lick Hattie's sleepy face. I'm almost surprised that she tastes the same as always. For some reason, I can't shake a strange feeling that something horrible almost happened . . .

Vwoop! Hattie unzips the blankets and takes

forever pulling on her clothes. She grabs a small paddle and gazes into it, grimacing and raking her fingers through her short hair like it's annoyed her. Clearly, she's perfectly safe, even if she's not happy at the moment.

But that's about to change. Because my nose detects the most wondrous aroma! And I hear the sounds of breakfast sizzling. "Great news, Hattie!" I bark, leaping and spinning. "I smell bacon!"

She clips on my leash, and we burst outside to the songs of cheerful birds. I spy Food Lady at the table pouring steaming coffee. Fetch Man stands by the Fire Space where the smoky bacon smell is coming from. After I water the big oak tree, we pause near the path, and I pick up an odor I can't identify—something sinister. My fur prickles.

As we get going again, I gaze around the clearing. On the other side of the tree, Muffin Lady and Tool Man are sipping from mugs while the ladies slurp from water dishes. Angel lopes toward us, munching an apple.

Across the clearing, Lucky is gobbling what sounds like crunchy kibble. Hammock Man stands over the wooden table stirring something in a large bowl. Beside him, Waddling Lady is painting June's cheek with a thin stick.

By the time I'm finished with my morning business, that horrible feeling of danger is long gone . . .

Until we hear a shriek from across the dirt road near the garbage bin. "Oh no!"

Everybody turns. Swirly-Arm Lady and Marcus are looking down at the ground, their faces shocked. Hot Dog Man appears behind them. "What the—?" he cries.

Clearly, something is wrong! Me and Hattie follow Food Lady as she rushes over. But before we even cross the road, I see the problem.

Their Food Box is on its side, food strewn on the ground. Everything's ripped apart or partially chewed—a torn bag of rolls, a ripped box of crumbly crackers, oozy smashed eggshells.

Angel and the ladies join us. "Looks like their food's been ransacked," Goldie mutters.

"Horrors!" Patches exclaims.

More humans rush over to the Food Box, gasping like they've never seen a mess before. Even Fetch Man and Food Lady, who've definitely seen plenty.

I have to find out who did this! But Hattie won't let me get closer. Stretching the full length of the leash, my nose begins sniffing. I've barely gotten started when a furious growl nearly freaks me out of my fur.

CHapter 7

Coco is staring me down, hackles up, teeth bared. "Get away from here, *Fenway!*" She spits my name like it's a yucky taste in her mouth. "Right now!"

Yikes! That dog can be pretty vicious when she wants to be. I jump back, my tail drooped.

Coco gets in my snout, her muzzle scrunched. "I'm in charge here," she snarls. "Not you."

I take another step back. "I'm only trying to help. I can sniff out who did this."

"I don't need any help from you." Coco whips around to face the ladies and Lucky, her eyes glowering. "Or anybody."

Lucky glances at the partially eaten food. "Ohmygosh! Ohmygosh!" he says. "Looks like somebody really chowed down! What're you gonna do, Coco? Huh? Huh?"

"Simple," she says, her tail perked. "I'm not going to do anything."

Are my ears playing tricks on me? Did she really say she's going to do nothing?

Whoever attacked this Food Box will probably strike again. We're clearly all in danger. I turn to the other dogs. Goldie's pawing at the ground. Patches is snapping at a fly. Lucky's gazing at Coco with huge eyes. They can't be okay with this, can they? Why aren't they questioning her?

"Not that I owe any of you an explanation," Coco says. "But I know my humans. Trust me, they're not going to leave food out again."

As if on cue, Swirly-Arm Lady lets out a loud sigh. Hot Dog Man squats beside the spilled food and starts tossing it into a black bag like the kind Fetch Man stuffs into the tall can in the garage.

Hey, wait a minute! Is Hot Dog Man throwing out perfectly good food? I spring up, my tail going nuts. It's bad enough that Coco isn't concerned about the wild animals, but now this?

"FEN-way," Hattie scolds, pulling me back.

I drop down in frustration. This is so unfair! In more ways than one!

Marcus comes up next to us, and Hattie pats him on the back. Angel does the same thing.

Some tall humans chatter with Swirly-Arm Lady while others help Hot Dog Man fill the bag.

"Why are you dogs still here?" Coco says with a sneer. "Don't you have anything better to do?" She whips around and struts off.

Lucky practically bounces after her. "Wait for me, Coco!" he yaps.

Goldie begins to follow, but Patches noses her to a stop. "Don't bother," she says in her lovely voice.

I leap up. Finally! "Ladies, we have to do something! We're under attack!"

"I hardly think so, Fenway." Patches nuzzles my fur.

"And besides," Goldie says, her ears flattened, "if the humans are more careful with their food, animals won't get into it."

They can't know that. None of us had a chance to check it out, thanks to Coco. The thief could be vicious and threatening and terrifying—or not. The truth is we have no idea who we're dealing with. How am I supposed to do my job?

I'm about to keep arguing with the ladies, but right then, Hattie pulls me over to the table.

Food Lady and Muffin Lady bring armfuls of food over to Marcus's family, and everybody chows down on pancakes and bacon. Hattie slips me a slice or two under the table. That's my girl!

Afterward, everybody gets busy. Marcus and Angel kick a ball around. The ladies curl up in the shade of the big oak tree. Coco grabs a stick, and Lucky chases her. Normally, I'd join in the game. But all I can think about are wild animals. I smelled them by the big oak tree, so they could have been near the Food Box, too. I have to keep Hattie safe.

She unties me from the table, and we wander across the clearing to the tall pine tree. June's seated cross-legged against the trunk, a book open on her lap. Hattie plops down next to her, and I cuddle up beside my short human.

She gazes at June's cheek. It's smudged again, but today it looks like a girl with wings. I've seen something like it before. "Nice-fair-ee," Hattie says.

June doesn't look up. "Thanks."

Hattie chatters and chatters while June keeps her mouth shut. When she turns the page, Hattie points. "Yoon-ih-corn," she says, her voice filled with admiration.

June smiles and flips to another page. In the corner, I spy a girl with wings. And that's when I realize where I've seen her before—in Hattie's notebook!

"Cool!" Hattie says.

I snuggle against Hattie's leg as the short humans chat. They're awfully interested in that book, even though it's not anything fun like a ball or a chew toy.

After a few minutes, Angel hurries over to us. She's cradling a black-and-white ball in one arm, the ladies right behind her. "Hattie," she cries, out of breath. "Wanna go to the Dog Park?"

My ears shoot up. So does my tail. Of course we want to go to the Dog Park! "Yippee!" I bark, romping across Hattie's lap. I don't see Marcus—or Coco—anywhere, but a group of other short humans is waiting and watching near the big oak tree. And the woodsy path that leads to the Dog Park.

Giggling, Hattie springs up. "You too?" she asks June.

I start leading Hattie toward the ladies. "Hooray! Hooray! We're going back to the Dog Park!"

Right then, we hear, "Ready, boy?" Hammock Man grabs an excited Lucky by the leash. He's got a bandanna around his head just like the one around Lucky's neck. They must spot a squirrel because the two of them take off into another trail in the woods, as if they've done this very thing hundreds of times.

Angel looks as impatient as I feel. "Hattie . . . the crew!"

"Come on," Hattie says, waving at June.

June's gaze falls back to the book. "Nah," she mutters, shaking her head.

Hattie glances at Angel, then over at the oak tree and the other short humans. Clearly, it's time to play! What's her hesitation? "See-ya," she says to June with a shrug. Finally!

The pine-y, mossy scents lead us down the same path as yesterday. Buzzes and chirps drift into my ears as they flap in the breeze. I see pawprints and hoofprints in the dirt, and I smell that strong, musky odor. It's everywhere!

Me and the ladies sprint most of the way. Turns out it's a good strategy for ignoring the snaky shadows on the brush, the gnawed-off tree trunk, and the dim sky full of treetops.

Hattie, Angel, and the rest of the short humans can barely keep up as we race to the gate. While we gasp for breath, we watch a single maple leaf drop off a low-hanging branch overhead and flutter to the ground.

A brown-and-white Corgi pokes his snout through a link in the fence. "New here?" he says, giving me a sniff-over.

"Nope," I say, thrusting out my chest. "I've been here since yesterday. The name's Fenway."

"Fenway?" He stares at me for a second with his head tilted, like he didn't just smell me or anything. "I've heard that name before somewhere."

"You were so right about this place," I tell the ladies. "So many dogs to play with! You come here every year? I could get used to this!"

Goldie looks like she wants to say something but changes her mind. Patches's eyes are kind as always. "We had a feeling you'd like it," she says.

The Dog Park is already humming with action. Dogs are crawling through the tube and climbing over the ramp and barking with glee as short humans laugh and chat and throw balls. "Hurry up, Hattie!" I bark. "I can't wait to play with my new friends!"

"The fun doesn't start without you, Fenway," Goldie says.

"Marcus!" a bunch of short humans shout as they rush toward him. As soon as Hattie opens the gate, we race inside.

"Whoopee!" I cry, shooting across the grass. The ladies are hot on my tail.

As I make a wide turn, I see Hattie and Angel dashing over to Marcus, who's surrounded by short humans.

He reminds me of Food Lady bossing us around. But for some reason, the rest of them don't seem to mind.

The ladies on my heels, I weave in, out, and around other dogs. Big, little, long-haired, short-haired—wowee! This must be the Most Popular Dog Park Ever!

"Hey, everybody!" I call, slowing as I approach the climbing ramp. "I don't want to brag or anything, but I used to be a champ on that thing back in the city."

A Wheaten Terrier stops mid-climb, her tags jingling. "Cool!" she cries. "Let's play follow the leader." She tells me her name is Kwanzaa.

"Yeah," says a dark brown Havanese with a little bow at his throat. He introduces himself as Hugo. "The more the merrier."

I lead the ladies up the ramp, the others trailing behind. "Check this out, guys!" I yell from the top. I leap into the air, spinning. "I'm flying!"

I hear Goldie's claws come to a clattering stop as I land. "Game over," she says.

"I hate to agree, but there's no way I am trying that move, Fenway," Patches says.

When I whirl around, everybody's frozen on the ramp. "Did you say his name was Fenway?" Hugo asks.

Kwanzaa cocks her head. "Um, I just remembered I have to go," she says, backing down the ramp.

Hugo scampers after her. "Kwanzaa, wait for me!"

I turn to Goldie and Patches, my ears wilting. "Why don't they want to play with me? Should I have tried an easier trick?"

The ladies exchange a glance. "Maybe," Patches says.

We tear around the perimeter of the Dog Park a few times. On the fourth or fifth round, I spy Coco strutting along the back fence, a line of other dogs tagging after her. I remember them from yesterday—Titan, Midnight, and Chorizo. Is that a new game? It looks pretty boring.

"Don't you ever get . . . tired, Fenway?" Goldie huffs as we near the front of the Dog Park. Again.

"He's got more energy than the rest of us put together!" Patches yells.

"Seriously . . . I need a break," Goldie says, puffing.

"Maybe a short one," I say, cruising up to the giant water dish. "Playing does make me thirsty." I plunge in for a good, long slurp. I hear the ladies come up beside me to do the same.

I must be drinking for longer than I thought. When I come up for air, two black-and-white dogs I don't know are suddenly guzzling right across from us. If I had to guess, I'd say the bigger one is a Border Collie and the other is a Boston Terrier.

"Hey," I say when they eventually look up. "You two seem like you'd be up for a challenge. Want to race me around the park?"

The Boston Terrier just stares. So does the Border Collie. Have they never seen such a handsome Jack Russell before?

Right when I'm beginning to wonder if the cat stole their tongues, the Boston cocks her head. "You're not that dog Fenway, are you?"

I stand a little taller, my tail high and waving. "I sure am!" I say. "Have you girls heard of me?"

The Boston looks at the Border Collie, who's already slinking away. "Um, sort of," she mutters. Next thing I know, she's skulking off, too.

My tail sinking, I turn to the ladies. "Nobody likes me. Do I smell flowery or something?"

Before they can respond, I notice Coco and her gang sauntering past, and suddenly, everything is crystal clear.

@Hapter 8

After we leave the Dog Park, we take a different path to a grassy field beside the pond. A group of humans—tall and short—is hanging around, like they're waiting for something exciting to happen. Unfortunately, me and the ladies get tied up under a huge elm tree. I have a terrible feeling we're about to miss out on the action.

"Whoa," I say to the ladies. "How many humans are here, anyway?"

"Too many to count," Goldie says. "More every year."

"Wait till the games begin," Patches says, sinking to the ground. "Get ready to hear lots of cheering."

Goldie rolls onto her side. "You mean yelling. These humans take play as seriously as you do, Fenway."

Heaving a sigh, I circle in place. "I knew we were going to be left out! Is Coco in charge of this, too?"

"That dog can be a real troublemaker," Goldie says, scratching behind her ear. "We warned you to be careful."

"But I was." I stretch out my front paws, pushing a couple of crispy leaves, then slump down on my belly. "I didn't do anything to her. Just being myself. And now nobody wants to be my friend."

"It's not you; it's her," Goldie gruffs. "She did the same thing to another dog last year. He was thirsty and drank out of her bowl. She made sure everybody knew about it."

"Poor thing became an outcast," Patches adds, gazing out over the busy field. "Notice he's not here this year. His humans, either."

"That's not fair." My hackles shoot up. "That Pomeranian shouldn't be able to get away with that stuff."

Patches looks up. "As if anyone could stop her."

I spring back onto my paws. "I won't let her sabotage my chances of making new friends."

"Nice thought, Fenway," Goldie says. "But how?"

I climb up and down over a fat root. "I don't know exactly." Or at all.

TWEEEEET-TWEEEEET! TWEET-TWEET-TWEET!

I pause mid-step, my head swiveling. "Yikes! What kind of bird was that?"

"Why, haven't you ever heard a whistle?" Patches asks.

Goldie cocks her head toward the field. "Check it out."

The humans suddenly go quiet, except for the tall man everybody's focused on. Coils of black hair seem to spring from his head, and he's holding a big cone in front of his mouth. His loud, distorted voice booms across the field. I can't understand a word he's saying—"teemz," "fass-tist," "prizez,"—and a whole bunch more.

Hammock Man is standing next to him, his arms wrapped around a basket. He's ditched the bandanna, his hair pulled back like before. Hot Dog Man comes up beside him, carrying a bulging sack.

As crowded as the field is, it's easy to spot My Hattie with her short hair and bouncy feet. She sure looks ready to play.

My tail droops, and I sink back onto my belly. What fun is a game without an enthusiastic dog?

Hattie glances around until she finds Angel. I spy other humans pairing off. Tall and short, dark-haired and light-haired—even Food Lady and Fetch Man seem to be getting ready to play. Although the look on Food Lady's face tells me she's not too sure she wants to.

Someone else looks like she doesn't want to play. June stands alone on the sidelines, her gaze fixed on the ground. Hammock Man walks over to her. He tugs at the braid hanging down her back and puts his arm around her shoulders.

Hattie must notice, because she dashes away from Angel and heads over to them. Her face still full of excitement, she chatters at June while nodding a lot. Kind of like when she's trying to coax me into eating something that tastes yucky. Like kibble that's totally different from the kind I usually eat.

Pretty soon, Hammock Man's expression is as encouraging as Hattie's. He taps June's back a few times. I can almost hear him saying, "Come on!"

Their convincing apparently works. Hammock Man leads June toward the big group while Hattie rushes back to Angel. The whistle tweets some more. The loud voice booms again. The humans scatter—half to one end of the field, half to the other. All at once, the humans on one side reach an arm out in front of their bodies.

I blink. "Are they holding spoons?"

Goldie bats at a fly. "Pretty sure they're trying to balance eggs. But there's no point in watching, Fenway.

Once they get started, this is impossible to figure out."

"I sort of get it," Patches says. "I think the goal is to share the egg. Or keep it from falling."

"But they don't eat it." Goldie sneers. "What kind of game is that?"

I finish licking my brown paw. "It does sound kind of boring. Even though I'd still rather play than be kicked out. I thought this was going to be a lot more fun."

"It's not easy to be on the sidelines," Goldie says.

Patches shoots her a look, then turns to me. "Just be patient, Fenway," she says in her lovely voice. "You'll figure out how to get along with Coco. After all, we did."

"Who says I want to?" I say. An extra fluffy caterpillar makes his way up and over the fat tree root. He's crawled partway up the elm's trunk when whoops and squeals and hollering draw my attention back to the field.

Some sort of race is going on. One group of humans with eggs on spoons walks very quickly toward the group on the far side of the field. I spy Angel rushing toward Hattie, whose eyes are huge, her hands reaching out. As if she cannot wait for Angel to give her that egg. Or spoon.

But not to eat? Goldie was right. This game makes no sense.

But the humans sure look and sound like they care

about it a lot. Some are jumping up and down. Others are screaming. Everybody seems totally pumped.

Loud whoops erupt as the first human arrives at the other end of the field and hands off her spoon—and egg. The other human grabs it and heads back across the grass, walking so fast he's almost running.

Marcus practically swipes the spoon from another boy and speed walks across the field, easily passing a bunch of others. One by one, egg-holding humans reach the waiting humans. Most pass the spoons, but one or two drop their eggs with a *splat*, followed by groaning.

Hattie screeches when she takes Angel's spoon. Angel, too. Hattie takes off!

As my short human hurries over the field, I can't help think she'd go much faster with a dog. My gaze is fixed on Hattie until I hear a gasp behind her.

A girl is down on the field. Hammock Man races over and pulls June to her feet. Her face is stunned. Her shirt is smeared with egg goo. She waves her arms, flicking her fingers as if they're covered with something icky. Like soapsuds.

"Oh, dear," Patches mutters.

"I saw that coming," Goldie murmurs. "She's not the type who wins games."

"Goldie!" Patches scolds. "That's not nice. I bet June

would win if the game involved reading books. Not every short human is the same."

"Neither are dogs," I add.

June pushes Hammock Man away and mopes off. By the time she gets to a cluster of trees, cheers erupt at the opposite end of the field.

Somebody starts a chant. "MAR-cus! MAR-cus! MAR-cus!" Marcus thrusts an arm overhead, and a bunch of short humans slap his hand. I don't need to understand the game to realize who just won.

Angel crosses the line moments after him.

While the humans keep shouting and cheering, me and the ladies drift in and out of sleep. Each time my eyes pop open, the humans are playing some other perplexing game. Two humans hobble-running with their legs tied together. Tossing balloons back and forth until one drops and somebody gets splashed with water. Humans hopping up and down with their legs inside a sack.

Finally, I see a game I know—tug-of-war. Except it's one group of humans on one end of the rope and the entire other group on the other. Weird as it looks, it seems they're pretty good at it. With all the groaning and straining and pulling, that rope is hardly moving at all.

"Gotta feel for them," Goldie says. How long has she been awake? "It's not like they can clench the rope in their strong canine jaws."

"But it's humans against humans," Patches points out. "So at least it's fair."

We watch until the rope moves enough that one side cheers while the other groans. The distorted voice with the cone booms. We hear a series of names called and more shouting and clapping and whooping. Then various humans stroll up to somebody who's handing out little bags that everyone seems to want.

If the scene was hectic before, it's even worse now. Humans chattering, romping back and forth, showing off their bags, heading in all directions.

It's not until I spy My Hattie racing over, her face full of joy, that I leap up. "Hooray! Hooray! I missed you so much!" I bark.

But before she gets to the elm tree, she slows. Making a turn, she rushes up to Hammock Man and June. For the first time, I notice she's carrying one of those small bags. She reaches in and pulls something out. A treat?

Hammock Man's face lights up, but June's gaze drops to her feet. She shakes her head.

Hattie looks discouraged. She hands the treat to Hammock Man, then pivots.

"I knew you'd come back!" I bark, leaping up and licking her hands as she unties me. She tastes sweet and fruity and nothing like a treat. Yuck!

Angel is already leading the ladies away. As we join them, Marcus bounds by with a group of others, laughing and sniggering, "I'm June—oof!" Then he pretends to fall on the ground.

What is it about him? I remember what the ladies said, "Like canine, like short human."

And that's when a question pops into my mind. A really big question.

CHAPTER 9

At first, I thought Coco was some sort of super alpha dog who has to be in charge. But now, I'm beginning to wonder if maybe there's another reason she wouldn't let me investigate that Food Box. "What's the deal with Coco?" I say as we trot along behind Hattie and Angel. When the short path ends, we walk along the dirt road. "Because I'm pretty sure she's up to no good."

Goldie snorts. "Fenway, if I had a bone for every time you said that about somebody. Let's see—the squirrels, the bunnies, the vet . . ."

Patches cocks her head like she's considering the possibilities. "Honestly, this time I'm not sure," she says. "If it were anyone but Coco, I'd say you're being overly suspicious. But there's not much I'd put past that dog."

Whoa! I don't know whether to feel comforted or worried. It's great that Patches is on my side. But she's the one always telling me to stop imagining the worst. If she thinks Coco is up to something, she definitely is!

The short humans chatter happily, reaching into their bags and popping treats into their mouths. Whatever those morsels are, they must be awfully chewy because Hattie and Angel are both chomping for a Long, Long Time. Normally, I'd ask for some, but that sweet, fruity smell is revolting.

Goldie nimbly hops over a rut in the road. "What are you saying, Fenway? That she's back at the campsite plotting to chew your favorite bone?"

Gulp! That would be awful! I give my head a good shake to clear out the despicable image. "No, actually, I was thinking of something much worse."

Patches turns to me, her eyes wide. "Oh my goodness. What could that be?"

"Well," I say, avoiding a hopping toad, "remember how Coco wouldn't let me or anybody else sniff around that knocked-over Food Box?"

Goldie scrunches her snout. "She had every right. It was her territory."

"What if she did it herself?" I check to make sure nobody's listening. "That's why she doesn't want to do anything about it."

"Fenway," Patches says, her voice kind and gentle. "Why would she do that? Her humans give her whatever she wants."

"And how could she knock over a box that big?" Goldie chimes in.

I come to a halt, little puffs of dust wafting up around my paws. "I don't know. Maybe she had help."

The ladies exchange a puzzled glance. Goldie speaks first. "Do you know how ridiculous that sounds?"

Patches gazes at me kindly. "It does sound rather unbelievable."

Hattie turns around. "Fenn-waay," she sings. "Come on." The inside of her mouth is darker than usual. It smells like really strong cherries.

"Well, in any case . . ." I whip around, my eyes bulging. "I think I need to find out more about that dog."

But first things first. At the end of the dirt road, we arrive at the clearing where we slept and ate—did Goldie call it the campsite? My tail swishes with excitement. Wonderful aromas of mustard and bread and cheese and—*mmmmm*—meat fill the air. This can only mean one thing—lunch! My mouth starts watering.

Marcus is sitting on top of the wooden table just beyond the garbage bin, his cheeks flushed and smiling. He holds out his bulging bag, proudly showing off its contents to Swirly-Arm Lady while she lays leafy lettuce on a slice of bread. He smells like the same sweet, fruity-ness as Hattie and Angel. Only way more of it.

Swirly-Arm Lady frowns at the bag, like maybe she feels the same way I do about fruit. She nods toward the backpack lying on the ground. I know that look. Clearly, she wants him to put those treats away.

When we get to the table where Fetch Man is busy spreading a plastic cloth, Hattie unhooks my leash. Lucky lumbers over to us. "Ohmygosh! Ohmygosh! You're back!" he yaps. "What'd I miss?"

Patches points her snout toward June and Hammock Man, who trudge in from the dirt road. His arm is around her shoulders. Her head is bowed down as if she can't take her eyes off her gooey shirt. "Your short human might need some attention, poor dear."

"Wow, is that egg?" says Lucky before bounding toward them. Little bits of dust fly up from the ground as he runs.

Hattie leaves Angel's side and rushes up to Hammock

Man, June, and Lucky as they head toward their pointy tent near the hammock and tall pine. Hattie's face is hopeful. "All-rite?" she asks.

June smiles weakly. Even from across the clearing, I can smell her unhappiness. She gives Hattie a little wave, then—*vwoop!*—disappears inside the pointy tent. Lucky clomps in after her. I can hear him give himself a good shake.

Hattie sighs and heads back to me and Angel. Little by little, the rest of the humans stream over to our table as Fetch Man sets out paper plates and Food Lady pours drinks from a thermos. Some of the humans are carrying trays that smell like tasty ham. Some are carrying bowls that smell like creamy potato salad.

Yum! When the humans sit down, I plop on my bum beside Hattie's sneakers. My tail thumps with anticipation. Have I mentioned how much I love picnics?

After my tummy is happily full of Hattie's crusts, I get to work on my plan. The humans are busy eating, the ladies are snoozing under the big oak tree, and best of all, Hattie seems to have forgotten my leash. This can only mean one thing—Opportunity.

I saunter up to Coco's campsite. The flaps of the boxy tent are wide open. Coco's inside, propped up in that bed like she owns the place. I poke my snout in. "Uh, hey there," I say, putting on my most friendly tone. "I forgot to say this before, Coco, but it's cool that you like to play Frisbee. Guess what? I have a Frisbee at home."

She cocks her head, like maybe she didn't hear me right. "You pushed your way into my tent to say you like Frisbee?"

"Well . . ." I sink my head onto my forepaws, my bum straight up. "We *both* like Frisbee."

She glares at me suspiciously. "Uh-huh."

"And so, um, I was thinking, since we're both Frisbee players and everything," I say, trying not to look her in the eye. "Maybe we could talk about stuff. Like those smells around the spilled food."

Coco huffs. She sounds like Goldie. "Why would I do that? I already said I don't need your help, *Fenway*."

I bow lower, swallowing the bad feeling in my throat. "I know. But two noses are better than one, right?"

"Nice try," she says, her eyes unfocused like she's bored. "But I have the situation under control. Notice there hasn't been another break-in."

I hop up onto all fours. "Come on, Coco. You should see me back home. When it comes to scaring off intruders, I'm a professional."

"The only intruder here is you." She yawns. "Now, go back to your own tent and keep your nose where it belongs."

"I'm not an intruder!" I yell.

She cocks her head, but her eyes look away as if completely uninterested.

My fur bristles. "I said I'm not an intruder!"

She lifts up her snout. "Huh-hhah-hhuh-hhah! That's a good one! You're really funny, you know? But who is in *whose* tent right now, uninvited?"

Whoa.

"Don't make me tell you to leave twice," she says.

Grrrrr! My whole body shakes with fury. I'm so mad, I could rip a chew toy to shreds! If there was any doubt before, now I know that Coco is definitely, positively, absolutely the Most Evil Dog Ever.

I'm about to snarl or snap or give her some other very vicious warning when we hear a shriek from behind the nearest table. "Hey! What the—!!!"

It's Marcus. And he sounds upset.

I whirl around and see Swirly-Arm Lady and Hot Dog Man rushing to Marcus. He's standing behind their wooden table, flushed and holding his backpack. I've seen it before, when he stashed his fruity treats inside. But it wasn't saggy and torn then.

Hattie and Angel head over, their faces full of alarm. And confusion. Hattie scoops me up. Clearly, she needs comforting. Good thing I'm here!

Swirly-Arm Lady's hand flies to her cheek. "Oh no!"

Hot Dog Man takes the backpack from Marcus. Bits of chewed wrappers fall out. "Lem-me-see."

Marcus balls his fists. "Who did it?"

My gaze zooms from Marcus to Coco to the tall humans and then back to Marcus again. I have a horrible feeling that we went through this same situation earlier today. But if Coco was inside her tent, it had to be someone else. My fur bristles with alarm.

The humans all start talking at once. Hot Dog Man examines the rip in the backpack. Marcus is seething. Hattie glances down at the scraps of paper in the dirt. Even from here I can smell how sweet and fruity they are.

This can only mean one thing—the thief is back! No wonder Hattie needs comforting.

On the far side of the commotion, I spy a dark shape coming out from behind the garbage bin. Lucky! He skulks around the humans, his tail between his legs, his bandanna untied and hanging limply from his neck. Where did he come from? Was he behind the table all this time?

CHAPTER 10

As the humans continue freaking out, Lucky perks up. "Ohmygosh! Ohmygosh!" he says, his tongue lolling to one side. "What's going on?"

Does he really not know? He was in the perfect position to see. Or smell. "Looks like somebody broke into Marcus's backpack," I say as he wanders up to me and Hattie. "And stole his treats."

Lucky looks surprised. "Well, that stinks." A soft breeze ruffles through the trees, and a pinecone lands—*plop!*—right beside him.

Hattie sets me down and clips on my leash. "Say, um, Lucky," I say. "Did you, um—see any . . . Hey, is that sap on your fur?" It smells kind of maple-y, but I can't really tell.

Lucky turns his neck, and his bandanna falls to the ground. He licks a sticky spot on his hind leg.

"Here." Hot Dog Man hands the ripped backpack to Marcus. Hot Dog Man's got the same expression Fetch Man gets when Hattie's left her sneakers outside all night. I wish Hattie would let me get closer so I could give it a sniff.

Marcus stomps over to the boxy tent. Coco shoots out of the opening just before he barges in.

She scuttles up to me and Hattie. "I know what you're up to, *Fenway*," she says with a sneer. I don't know if it's my imagination, but her fur is poofed out even more than usual.

I gape at her. "You do?"

Coco raises her snout. Even though I'm twice as tall as she is, I get the feeling she's not doing it so she can look up to me. "Nosing around where you don't belong? Again?"

"Me and Lucky were chatting."

Coco bares her teeth and growls. "Sure you were. Now beat it!"

Before I can respond, Hattie snatches me away from Coco. I swear I see Lucky lurking behind the pointy tent, calm as can be. If he knows something or saw something, he's sure not acting like it.

Hattie heads across the dirt road to our table, where Food Lady and Fetch Man are cleaning up, leading me farther and farther away from the scene of the crime. Coco's shrill voice yips after me. "Mind your own business, *Fenway*!"

Fetch Man holds open a big plastic bag, and Food Lady stuffs delicious-smelling paper plates and napkins and cups inside. Hattie deposits me under the bench and starts to help. I do my part by licking yummy mayonnaise off her fingers.

"Fenway," she says with a sigh. Clearly, she doesn't want any help.

"Why'd you bring me over, then?" I whine, sinking down in the dirt. I'm trying not to think about Coco. Wish I knew what her deal was.

Beyond our tent, I spy Goldie and Patches stretching in front of the big oak tree. Hooray! They're finally awake! I realize my leash isn't attached and decide to head over.

"'Sup, ladies?" I say, dashing between them, my leash dragging behind me. "I need to ask you something. About that Chocolate Lab."

But they're not paying attention. They obviously have something else on their minds. I follow their gazes to Angel, who's filling water bottles from a spout on the other side of the clearing. Then to their tent as Tool Man and Muffin Lady pop out holding chunky-looking boots.

Goldie's ears sag. "Oh no!" she moans. "They're not leaving us alone again?"

The ladies are quiet a moment as we watch the tall humans stuff their feet into the boots and lace them up. Angel returns with the bottles, swatting at a fly. Muffin Lady tosses her a can of choky spray.

"Not so fast, Goldie," Patches says, her tail coming to life. "I think we're going on a hike!"

Goldie brightens. "It's about time! I hope we can collect sticks."

"Certainly!" Patches cries. "Finding sticks is one of the best parts about hiking. Besides all the sniffing spots, of course."

Suddenly, Goldie's as animated as a puppy. She kicks up a couple of leaves as she romps around. "Yes! I can hardly wait!"

My tail droops. I hate it when my friends are leaving.

"Why so sad, Fenway?" Patches says, giving me a playful nudge. "You'll love hiking. It's like a long, long walk."

My ears shoot up. "I'm going, too?"

"Everybody is!" Patches's snout gestures toward my family's campsite. Food Lady's putting on a cap just like

Fetch Man's. Three water bottles are lined up on the wooden table. That choky spray, too.

"Yippee!" I yell, leaping and twirling. "I'm so ready! I'm so ready!"

Marcus bounds over as Angel pulls a fat tail of hair through the back of her cap. He offers her some shiny apples that she stuffs in her backpack. Both short humans are wearing laced-up boots like Tool Man's and Muffin Lady's. Marcus says something to Angel, and she throws her head back, laughing.

As I glance around the clearing, I don't see Hattie. She must be inside the tent changing her clothes. Again.

Swirly-Arm Lady helps fasten a backpack on Hot Dog Man's back. I turn to the ladies. "Hey, if they're going, too, does that mean Coco—?"

"Hold on," Goldie says, her voice mysterious.

Patches gazes up at the sky. "Just wait and see."

Before I can even ask, Swirly-Arm Lady lifts the Pomeranian in all her poofy-ness. The sun glints off Coco's sparkly collar as the lady human tucks her into the backpack. Hot Dog Man's going to carry her on the hike?

The ladies exchange smirks.

I'm about to ask if this is a joke when Hattie emerges from the tent. I gallop over to her. "Hooray! Hooray!" I bark, pawing her legs. "I love hiking!"

Hattie stoops down and picks up my leash. Food Lady tries to hand her the choky spray, but she doesn't take it. Instead, she shakes her head. "Not going."

Food Lady looks concerned. "Why not?"

Hattie doesn't answer. She gazes across the clearing, to where June is sitting by herself against the pine tree. That book is open on her lap again.

Food Lady kisses Hattie's cheek. "Nice," she says.

I'm not sure what that was all about, but I'm getting the feeling we're going to miss out on the hike. I'm feeling disappointed until I sense opportunity—with Coco gone, maybe I can find out what happened to that backpack.

Marcus and Angel rush up. Marcus offers Hattie an apple and looks her over, his forehead scrunching. "Ready?" he asks.

"Not going." Hattie looks away.

"What?" Angel cries, her eyebrows arching under the bill of her cap.

Hattie shrugs, her gaze drifting over to June.

Marcus glances across the clearing and frowns. "Come on, Hattie," he says, slapping her shoulder. "The crew!"

She hangs her head. "Nah."

"June-ih-corn June?" Marcus says. He jabs Angel in the side.

"No," Hattie says in a meek voice.

Marcus looks stunned. "What?" he asks Hattie, like maybe he didn't hear what she said.

Hattie makes a pained face and rubs her belly. "Sick," she says, even though she smells perfectly fine.

"Oh no," Angel says in a sad voice.

"Let's go!" Hot Dog Man calls, waving his arm. Coco on his back, he and Swirly-Arm Lady head to the trail just past the garbage bin where Hammock Man and Lucky went running. Tool Man and Muffin Lady hurry by with the ladies. Fetch Man and Food Lady line up behind them. Hammock Man rounds out the group, the shiny rings on his ears sparkling in the sun.

Angel looks at Hattie with hopeful eyes. "Feel better."

"Lay-ter," Marcus says as he and Angel rush over to the tall humans and dogs. And Coco. I watch them disappear through the trees.

Me and Hattie stroll over to June. She plops down. "Hey."

June glances up, an actual smile spreading across her face. Soon the short humans are focused on the book and chattering away.

Finally, it's my chance to do some investigating! I decide to start with Lucky. He's curled up lazily near Waddling Lady, who's dabbing paint on a propped-up board. And Hattie's dropped my leash.

I saunter over to him. "So, what's going on?" I say as casually as possible. "Too full to move?"

Lucky raises his head. "Huh?" He couldn't look more innocent.

"I was just thinking. You look awfully content. Like maybe you chowed down a little too much, if you know what I mean?"

"Ohmygosh, I get that a lot," he says. "But it's all muscle, seriously. I'm a lot stronger than you'd think."

I'm about to ask him another question when Hattie and June hurry over to Waddling Lady.

"Sure," she says, grinning from under her floppy hat. She grabs a different brush and starts painting on Hattie's cheek.

I scamper to Hattie's side to watch. She smells excited. June reaches down and pats the top of my head, her long braid swinging over her shoulder.

Caw-caw-caw! A loud bird sounds from someplace way-up-high. A crow? He sounds angry or urgent, like he's giving us a warning.

June stands back, gazing at Hattie's cheek. Right in the center is a horse's head with a glittery horn coming out of its forehead. "Awesome!" June cries, clapping her hands.

Hattie opens her mouth like she's going to say

something. But right then, we hear a rustling sound and footsteps thudding into the campsite. We all turn.

Marcus is out of breath as he sprints to the table. He grabs the lone water bottle and whirls around. His eyes widen as he sees us. "Hattie?"

Chapter 11

Hattie leaps up, gasping. She takes a few steps toward Marcus. "Um, hey!" she cries, her hand on her face. She turns the painted cheek away from him. Clearly, she's startled.

Sweeping a curl off his sweaty forehead, he strides across the campsite. He gazes sideways at Hattie and June. "Sick?" he asks, his voice sounding skeptical.

Hattie glances at June, then back at Marcus. She looks away, like she does when she's nervous. Or uncomfortable. "I—uh, I . . ." she stammers.

Waddling Lady wipes her paintbrush on a cloth. June watches like it's the most fascinating thing she's ever seen.

"Um, better," Hattie says, patting her belly. A soft breeze ruffles her short hair.

Marcus squints and points at Hattie's face. "Yoon-ih-corn?" he asks, his face puffed out like he's about to burst into laughter.

"What—uh . . ." Hattie pulls a tissue from her pocket and swipes at her cheek.

"Well, come on," he says, turning to go. The water bottle swings from his finger.

Hattie mutters, "Yeah—okay." She glances back at June, whose eyes look surprised and sad at the same time.

Hattie swivels around and grabs my leash. We rush across the campsite.

My tail goes nuts. We're going on the hike after all! But then my tail droops when I realize I've lost my chance to question Lucky and investigate the crime scenes. For now.

As we hurry after Marcus, Hattie turns and offers a little wave to June. She's already slumped against the pine tree, her face buried in the book. Lucky drops down at Waddling Lady's feet like he's too sluggish—or full—to move.

The ladies were right about the hike—it was just a long walk. But they must have forgotten to warn me about the wild animal scents. I spent the whole hike with my hackles up. And I must've scared those creatures away with my ferocious presence because even the squirrels and chipmunks kept their distance.

At suppertime, everybody heads back down the dirt road to the field where the humans played games with eggs, sacks, and ropes. But this time, there are long tables that smell like yummy food—fried chicken, buttery corn on the cob, and sweet, crumbly corn bread!

My tongue drips out of control. "Wowee!" I say to the ladies as Hattie and Angel pull us over to one of the tables. "I love corn bread!"

Patches sniffs the air. "It is rather delicious," she says.

"Don't get too excited, Fenway," Goldie says as the short humans fiddle with our leashes.

Next thing I know, me and the ladies are tied up at the far end of the table while our short humans slide onto the benches. Suddenly, all I hear are loud voices and laughter. I sink onto my paws, trying to ignore the tantalizing smells.

I glance around for Food Lady and Fetch Man. They're seated at one of the far tables, chattering away with a bunch of other tall humans. When I turn back, I realize our table is loaded with short humans—noisy, jostling, rowdy short humans. "The crew," I catch somebody say.

Goldie drops down for a scratch. "They have more energy than bunnies," she says as if reading my thoughts.

"I'd say they're more like puppies," Patches says. "Squirming, yapping, pushing."

I rest my snout on my forelegs. Why do short humans get to have all the fun—not to mention tasty food—while dogs have to be cooped up with nothing to do?

The ladies slump down beside me in the soft, cool grass. Patches licks her hind leg. Goldie yawns. She looks like she's too bored to move.

The image of another lazy dog swims into my mind. "Hey, ladies," I say, perking up. "How long have you known that Chocolate Lab?"

Patches stops mid-lick. "Lucky?"

"Since always," Goldie says. "Why?"

I lean my head against the table leg. "He's pretty tough, right?"

"Look at him," Goldie mutters. "He's massive."

"Why do you ask?" Patches says as a fly buzzes around her ear.

"I was just thinking." I give my head a shake. "He was right there when Marcus's backpack was broken into. And he's big enough to knock over a Food—" I lose the thought as the mouthwatering aroma of fried chicken hits my nose. It's all I can do to stop drooling.

"Look, Fenway," Patches says, snapping me out of my chicken-y dream. "I hope you're not accusing Lucky of anything. He's as laid-back as they come. I can't even imagine him taking something that wasn't his."

"What about last year?" Goldie says to Patches. "When June spilled that ice cream? He was all over it."

Patches scowls, pawing at a squashed pinecone in the grass. "So? We would've done the same thing."

Goldie sighs. "I'm just saying."

Patches has a point. Every dog knows spilled ice cream is fair game. And somehow June seems like the type of short human that would happen to. I think of her falling on that egg during those strange field games. "Hey, where *is* June?"

Goldie points her snout toward the next table.

I crane my neck. It's crowded like all the other tables, except at one end there's a short human sitting quietly with her head down. I don't have to see her up close to know it's June with her eyes in a book. It probably has "yoon-ih-corns" in it. I think of Hattie's cheek and wonder why she wiped the paint off.

When it's completely dark and the crickets are chirping, me and Hattie snuggle up inside the tent. She smells like mint and vanilla and marshmallow. "Aw, Fenway," she says, patting my head. She pulls out a flashlight and that notebook from under her pillow.

Hooray! Comm-ix! I can't wait for another story!

I nuzzle against Hattie's shoulder as she makes lines and curves on the paper. Her picture looks like a horse's head with a long horn. And a girl with delicate wings.

As she draws, Hattie whispers to me. I don't understand what she's saying, but her words sound jumbled. Her face is scrunched up like she's anxious. Or unsure.

After a while, she must get tired because she tucks the notebook away, and the flashlight goes out. She lays her head on the pillow and hugs me tight.

I'm pretty tired myself. But there's no way I'm closing my eyes.

Creepy voices are chirping. Powerful wings are thwapping. I could've sworn I caught a strange gamy odor when we came back from dinner. And the woods are right on the other side of the tent.

I have to stay on guard. I have a short human to protect. I'll stay alert all night if I have to. Nothing is more important than keeping Hattie safe. Especially now, when she's so upset. Clearly, she's afraid of sleeping so close to those wild animals for another night. They could've already struck once. Or twice! The rodents and birds smell bad enough, but every now and then I catch a musky whiff of strange creatures I can't identify. Will they slink out of the woods with evil on their minds? Again?

Hattie needs me now more than ever. I cuddle up tighter against her as her breathing slows. Her minty, vanilla-ish pillow is so inviting, I lay my head down. Just for a second.

My body calms. All of a sudden, I'm out in the grass with the buzzing insects. My ears up and my tail out, no creature wants to mess with me. I'll patrol the campsite forever if that's what it takes!

Footsteps pad on the pine needles, twigs snapping. Are they headed this way? I strain to listen, my whole body shaking. Jingling. Jangling. Dog tags?

I leap out, my tail swooshing. New friends are here to play!

A three-legged German Shepherd, a big black Poodle, and a Dachshund run through the grass. A brown-and-white Corgi, a curly-haired Wheaten, and a dark brown Havanese with a little bow tie romp out from between two pine trees. Two black-and-white dogs—a Border Collie and a Boston Terrier—prance around the big oak.

I sprint toward them. "Hey, everybody! It's me—Fenway!

Want to go to the Dog Park? There's a cool climbing ramp and an awesome crawling tube!"

The Wheaten, Kwanzaa, pulls to a stop, cocking her head. "We don't play with intruders!"

The Border Collie glares at me. "You need to mind your own business."

My ears droop and I back away. I was only trying to be friendly.

The dogs gather around, murmuring. Are they talking about me?

The Dachshund, Chorizo, nudges to the front of the pack. "Fenway nosed around where he doesn't belong, right?"

Hugo the Havanese scowls. "Nobody wants to play with you."

"We're not friends with Fenway," chorus the others. And they start to head off in every direction.

"Wait!" I go to stop them, but there are tons of them and only one of me! "I'm nice. I swear!"

In a split second, I'm alone. With the trees and the crickets.

My heart feels heavier than a boulder. Why don't they believe me?

Another dog pops out of a backpack. Moonlight glints off her sparkly collar. Her eyes stare at mine, forcing me to look away.

"Go away!" Coco yells. "I didn't invite you here."

I have to get away. If only I could stop whimpering . . .

"Surprise!" *booms another voice. Lucky?*

He bounds out of the woods, his bandanna dangling from his neck. "Ohmygosh! Ohmygosh, Fenway!" *he cries.* "We can romp through the woods and make friends with vicious animals. They're not afraid of me! And they won't be afraid of you, either. We can watch them steal stuff from our families!"

"NO!" *I moan, reversing direction.* "You've got it wrong, Lucky."

"Get lost, Fenway!" *Coco howls.* "Nobody likes you."

"Yes, they do," *I whine.* "Hattie likes me. I'm here to protect her. And make her happy. Because she's worried. And anxious. And—"

I turn one way. Lucky grins and slobbers.

I turn the other way. Coco stares me down.

I'd leave, but I'm surrounded. So I burrow under the pine needles as deep as I can. They smell like mint and vanilla. And marshmallows.

CHapteR 12

The aroma of smoky bacon wakes up my nose. I crawl out from under the blanket and onto Hattie's chest. "Get up! Get up!" I bark, licking her chin. "It's breakfast time outside!"

"Aw, Fenway," she says, her eyes fluttering open. Smiling, she gives me a scratch behind the ears.

Just like yesterday, it takes her longer than usual to pull on her clothes. It's almost as if she can't decide which shirt to wear. Aren't they the same? I start to wonder if this is how it's going to be from now on. "Come on, Hattie!" I bark, my tail swishing. "We're missing out on the bacon!"

Finally, after running her fingers through her hair a whole bunch of times, she unzips the tent—*vwoop!*—and we charge outside. Even though the sun is shining, the air feels cooler. A bird *peck-peck-pecks* in a tree overhead. Fetch Man is taking the Food Box out of the car. Food Lady sits at the wooden table sipping from a steaming mug. Hattie rushes over.

Normally, I'd go, too, but the smell of eggs and bacon lures me to the next campsite. Angel and Tool Man are standing over a sizzling Fire Space while Muffin Lady pours coffee and the ladies slurp thirstily from their water bowls.

I bound over to check out the yummy aromas. Angel pulls a plastic bag out of a Food Box. *Mmmmm!* Even before she opens it, I know it's bacon! I leap on Angel's leg, my tongue drooling with desire. "Hey, Angel! Don't you want to share that bacon with your good buddy?"

She giggles and shoos me down. "Off, Fenway!"

I hang my head. It was worth a try.

Hattie must hear because she charges over. "Fenway!" She smells annoyed. "FEN-way, no!" she snaps.

Like I didn't already get the message. Avoiding what I'm sure are her angry eyes, I wander over to Goldie and Patches. I hear her say "sorry" to Angel and Tool Man.

"'Sup, ladies?" I say, giving them each a friendly sniff.

"It's about time you got up," Goldie says, lifting her head from a water dish. Foamy water drips off her whiskers.

"We've already been to the Dog Park and back," Patches says.

"What?" I surprise myself with a shudder. "How-how was it? Was everybody, um, friendly?"

"Oh, Fenway," Patches says in her kind voice. She gives me a gentle nudge. "Don't let Coco get to you. Any dog would want to be your friend once they get to know you."

Good old Patches. She's always so encouraging. But she doesn't realize how bad it feels when other dogs call you names. "I don't know about that," I say. "Maybe it was good that I missed out."

Goldie gulps down more water. "Actually, the place was practically empty."

My ears perk up. "Really?"

Patches nudges me again. "Try not to worry, Fenway," she says. "Things usually work themselves out if you're patient."

I look at her sideways. Easy for her to say.

I'm about to go over to the Fire Space and see Tool

Man and Angel about that bacon when I hear Hattie's voice across the clearing. She's sitting under the pine tree with June, nibbling something. A granola bar? I love granola bars!

I romp over, my tail going nuts. My tongue starts dripping as I pick up the scent of peanut butter. My favorite! "How about sharing?" I bark, climbing onto her lap.

Hattie gives me a scowl-y look, but she still tosses a crumble into my mouth. *Mmmmm!* As I chew, I notice she's given June her drawings from last night. She must've ripped a page out of the notebook.

June wraps her long braid around her finger as she takes the paper. "Thanks," she mutters, not looking up. She folds the page and tucks it into her pocket.

Hattie smiles. She smells relieved, like the time she brought that bunny back to the neighbors across the street.

Waddling Lady waddles over, her hand pressed to her lower back. She speaks to June, and I catch a few words I know—"Lucky" and "Dog Park."

June frowns, but Hattie smiles. "Yeah!" she says, getting to her feet as I hop off her lap. "Let's go."

We're going to the Dog Park before breakfast?

Next thing I know, June and Lucky follow me and

Hattie down the path by the big oak tree. I hear the ladies call from behind, "Good luck, Fenway!"

Spooky, wispy light glows through the pine trees like sprays of water. A gnarled branch hovers over me as if it's a claw about to strike. Loud chitters and squawks sound as a couple of nasty squirrels clatter up a tree. My hackles bristle. These woods are full of danger. And after all the strange scents I've picked up lately, I'm not too excited about going along this trail.

Not to mention the unwelcome reaction from the park full of dogs at the other end.

June strolls ahead of Lucky, walking shoulder to shoulder with Hattie. The girls chatter about "yoon-ih-corns" and "fair-ees." For once, I notice June's not clutching her book. She actually sounds happy.

Lucky, on the other paw, sounds happy all the time. "Ohmygosh! Ohmygosh!" he says, his tail swaying back and forth. "Are you ready to romp?"

"Um, yeah," I say, avoiding his gaze. Until I know for sure if he had anything to do with what happened to those treats, I have to stay alert around him. Plus, we're not out of the woods yet.

As we close in on the Dog Park, the yipping and yapping and barking tell me it's way more crowded than the ladies said. My fur prickles.

I can't help but notice Coco. She's smaller than most of the other dogs, but somehow she's the most visible. Maybe it's her poofy-ness. Maybe it's the dogs following her around. Or maybe she just has a way of commanding attention.

Once we're inside, Hattie and June slide onto the bench near the front gate. Lucky takes off, his bandanna flapping in the breeze. I'm in a Dog Park full of dogs and short humans, but suddenly I'm alone. I wander over to the giant water dish and start lapping, even though I'm not thirsty.

I hear jingling dog tags nearby. Should I glance up? Should I say hi? My tail sags and curls against my bum.

Dog voices murmur. Are they saying "that's him" and "he's the one"? Or is it my imagination?

By the time I have the courage to look, the dogs are gone. Or maybe they were never there.

The Dog Park is hopping with dogs climbing on the ramp, crawling through the tube, chasing balls and Frisbees. Coco is in the middle of it all, leading every game and not sticking with any of them for more than a few seconds. Wherever she goes, the rest of the dogs follow.

My heart thuds. This is not the way it's supposed to be. But I know if I romp over there and try to join in, the other dogs will suddenly remember they have something else to do. Or worse.

The breeze ripples the leaves in that low-hanging branch of the maple tree. I see some short humans gathered under it. They're all focused on one, who seems to be chatting and gesturing while the others look on, laughing and bumping fists. The crew. Even from here at the water dish, I know the leader is Marcus. He's always the leader. And he's up to no good. *Like canine, like human.*

I've never not known what to do before. Especially in a Dog Park. But I can't keep slurping water all day. I look around for other options.

Dogs, short humans, more dogs, more short humans—Hattie! Why didn't I think of her right away?

I scamper over to the bench where she and June are sitting. "Hattie! Hattie!" I bark, pawing her leg. "Let's play chase!"

"Aw, Fenway," she sings, patting my head and turning back to June. She does not get up.

I cock my head. Hattie loves to run and play. Did she really come to the Dog Park to sit on a bench? Maybe she needs more convincing. "Come on, Hattie!" I paw her leg again. More forcefully this time. "Don't you want to play with your adorable dog?"

"Shhh, Fenway," she mutters, her focus still on June. I hear her say "drag-un" and "fly-ing" and a stream of other words I don't know. How can words be more interesting than romping around? Especially with her best buddy.

I have to convince her. I gaze up with my biggest, saddest eyes. "How can you resist this cute face?" I whine.

"Awww," she says, thrusting out her lower lip. She reaches down and scoops me into her arms. She hugs me tight.

Being in Hattie's arms is one of my all-time favorite places to be. But we can cuddle anywhere. Doesn't she realize we're in the Dog Park? Where are her priorities?

I'm about to wiggle out of her grasp when I hear the group of short humans headed this way. Led by Marcus, they're squirming and jostling more than I ever could.

"Hey, Hattie," Marcus says. He reaches his arm across June, his palm open.

Hattie's breathing quickens and she smells worried. She smiles weakly and slaps his hand. "Hey, Marcus," she mutters.

There's something about that Marcus I don't trust. "Keep your distance!" I growl.

Hattie gasps. "FEN-way!" she scolds.

Marcus jumps back, his arms flailing. "Help! Help! A puppy!" he yells, laughing.

The rest of the short humans laugh, too. I don't get the joke, but it feels familiar somehow.

Hattie's cheeks get hot. She smells even more worried than before. She turns away.

Marcus waves his hand in front of Hattie's face. "Cah-new-trip!" he says, which must be some sort of rallying cry because the other short humans suddenly start whooping and hollering. They gather around the bench, practically pressing in on us.

"Come on, Hattie," one of them says.

"Yeah, Hattie," another one says.

"The crew!" says another. He gives Hattie's shoulder a little shove. "The crew!"

Hattie glances at June, whose brow is scrunched up. Hattie forces a smile. "Cah-new-trip?" Hattie murmurs.

June frowns. Clearly, she's not interested in whatever Hattie asked her about.

Marcus waves his hand at Hattie again. *"Yoon-ih-corn???"* He says it the way Coco says my name. With disgust.

June slouches lower on the bench. Her scent is a mixture of doubt and fear.

Marcus folds his arms across his chest and rocks back on his heels. "Come on, Hattie."

"Yeah, Hattie," some of the others say. "Come on."

"Come on, Hattie!" the rest of them shout.

A few start clapping their hands and chanting. "Hat-tie, Hat-tie, Hat-tie!" Pretty soon they're all doing it. "Hat-tie, Hat-tie, Hat-tie!"

Hattie wraps her arms around me even tighter, her heartbeat thudding in my ear. Obviously, she needs some comforting. I nuzzle against her cheek. It feels hot again.

Right then, Lucky comes bounding over and leaps on June. "Ohmygosh! Did you see what I did?" he yaps. "I ate a whole stick!"

What—he ate a stick? Will the guy eat just about anything? Like those chewy fruity treats?

Hattie hops off the bench. "Ready?" she says to June, setting me down.

As June pushes Lucky off and grabs his leash, Hattie turns to Marcus. "Maybe," she mutters. Then we head out the gate.

@HAPTER 13

All the way back to the clearing, Hattie and June chatter about "yoon-ih-corns" again. It's good to have my calm, happy Hattie back. That Marcus is nothing but trouble. No wonder she was so worried when he showed up.

When we get to our campsite, June and Lucky head across to join Waddling Lady, who's pouring drinks from a thermos. Hattie waves after them. "See-ya," she calls.

Hattie rushes to the wooden table, and I leap onto the bench, my nose going nuts. *Sniff, sniff . . .* pretzels. "I'll take one of those!" I bark, reaching my nose toward them.

Hattie pulls me into her arms. "No-no-no!"

Food Lady and Muffin Lady are seated across from

each other holding cards out like fans. They're completely engrossed, like they're watching for an evil squirrel to make its move.

Hattie stuffs a pretzel into her mouth. "Cah-new-trip," she says to the tall humans.

"Mmm-hmm," Food Lady says, picking up a card from the pile.

Just then, Angel comes sprinting over. Under her cap, her eyes and cheeks are grinning. The sun glitters on something metal that swings from a string around her neck.

"Whoa!" Hattie says, trying to grab it. I hear a rattling sound from inside the metal. It sounds familiar. "Cool-wiss-el!"

Angel laughs and swats Hattie's hand away. "Safe-tee," she says. She puts it up to her lips and blows. *Tweet-tweeeeet!*

Yow! I try to bury my head in Hattie's shirt. Is that thing ever loud!

Food Lady must not mind the piercing noise. She says a whole bunch of words to Hattie in a warning voice. I hear "safe-tee" a few more times.

Hattie nods a lot and smiles at Angel. They slap hands.

Then Food Lady gets up from the table holding a can, and I turn my head. It's the spray that makes me choke!

That's my cue. I leap out of Hattie's arms. As I land in the dirt, little clouds of dust swirl up around me.

I scamper a safe distance away. Hattie turns all the way around, Food Lady spraying her arms and legs and the back of her neck.

Ew! Even from here, that stench is horrible! It makes no sense that Food Lady coats Hattie in dog repellant before she goes outside after supper or here in the woods. Doesn't she know that Hattie needs me to keep her safe? Between the wild animals and that trouble-maker Marcus, I can't let her out of my sight.

Muffin Lady fills the water bottles again while the short humans chatter excitedly. It sure seems like she and Angel are getting ready to go somewhere, and I'm getting a terrible feeling about it.

The feeling gets worse when at the next campsite over, I see Swirly-Arm Lady stuff Coco into Hot Dog Man's backpack and call, "Bye!" to Marcus. As they head into the woods, Marcus grabs a water bottle and hurries toward us.

I stand my ground. "Oh, no, you don't!" I bark as he rushes up. "If you think you're going somewhere with Hattie, you'll have to get through me!"

"Wah!" he cries, his eyes bulging for a moment before he bursts out laughing. He sidesteps me and charges up to Hattie and Angel. "Ready?" he asks.

"Ready!" Hattie and Angel say at the same time.

What? I knew something like this would happen. I scamper over and run circles around Marcus's feet. Instead of sneakers, he's wearing rubbery sandals. "Stay away from my short human," I snarl.

"Fenway, stop!" Hattie scoops me up. She hands me to Fetch Man as he comes out of the tent.

I wiggle and kick. "Let me go!" I bark, but Fetch Man tightens his grip.

"Have fun!" Food Lady calls as the short humans head away from the clearing.

"Are you nuts?" I bark, squirming in Fetch Man's arms. "That guy is trouble. And now Hattie doesn't have her protector!"

I keep up the warnings and protests, but it's no use. Fetch Man clips on my leash and ties me to the table leg. This is the Worst Thing Ever! Hattie is gone, and I'm stuck here with the tall humans. Trapped and doing nothing. I can't even use the opportunity to sniff for clues about the stolen food.

I sink down on my belly and moan. My gaze drifts across the campsite. June emerges from the pointy tent, her long braid dangling over her shoulder. Her book under her arm, she strides up to our campsite.

Food Lady looks up. "Hey, June," she says, smiling.

June looks puzzled. I hear her ask something about Hattie.

"Oh," Food Lady says, her expression falling. "Cah-new-trip."

Now June's face is the one that falls. "Oh." Her tone is sad. So is her scent. Is she just as disappointed as I am that Hattie left?

June rushes back and disappears inside her tent like she's being chased. Lucky and Hammock Man bound out seconds later. Hammock Man has that bandanna around his head again. He grabs Lucky's leash, and they take off into the woods the way they did the other day.

Well, this stinks. Hattie's in a dangerous situation without her loyal dog to watch out for her. Marcus is probably going to jump out of a tree again and scare her. Or chant her name and make her feel worried. Maybe I haven't spotted the wild animals, but I sure can spot Marcus. He's just as much of a threat to my short human!

Food Lady walks around the table, and I spring into action. "Please!" I bark, leaping and twirling. "We have to find Hattie. Before it's too late!"

"FEN-way," she snaps.

My tail droops. But then Fetch Man appears and takes the leash. "Wanna go for a walk?" he says.

"Haven't you been listening?" I bark, jumping on his legs. "Yes, I want to go for a walk!"

Right then, the ladies saunter up with Tool Man and Muffin Lady. My ears shoot up. Whoopee! Do they have the same idea?

"Calm down, Fenway," Goldie says as we start to head out of the clearing. "You're acting like you've never gone on a walk before."

"Who could blame him?" Patches says in her gentle voice. "The pond *is* awfully exciting."

I give my head a shake. "Did you say we're going to the pond?" My mind fills with images of picnics with Nana and games of fetch in the grass. Under other circumstances, those are a lot of fun. But right now, all I care about is finding Hattie. Is she at the pond?

Birds chirp overhead as we make our way down the dirt road. "The pond is where the canoes are," Patches explains as we walk around a pile of acorns. "Our precious Angel loves floating on the water. Last year, she paddled around the pond for most of one afternoon!"

My fur tingles. Is Hattie in the water? A twig snaps under my brown paw. Suddenly, I remember something. "So, ladies! I've got a theory about Lucky."

Goldie cocks her head. "What is it?"

"At the Dog Park," I say, practically hopping on the

pine needles as the words fly out of my mouth. "He ate a stick!"

The ladies exchange glances. Patches looks away first. "So?"

It figures the ladies are slow to catch on. They don't put clues together the way I do. They are not professionals.

"I know you don't think Lucky stole those yucky treats, but if he likes eating sticks, he'd probably eat anything."

"Look, we're here!" Goldie announces as we arrive at the field. Up ahead, I see a pond with a little house beside it. Way off to one side, I can just make out the Dog Park.

"Fenway, wait until you see this," Patches says. We head through the soft grass to the edge of the water.

My tail starts to wag hopefully when the tall humans mention Hattie and Angel. Apparently, they want to find them, too. Thank goodness they listened to me!

I pull to a stop in the wet sand before tiny waves can lap onto my paws. My head swivels. "Where's Hattie?"

Patches points her snout toward the water. "Out there," she says. "See those canoes?"

I stretch as far as I can on the leash, squinting. A

bunch of boats—canoes?—are out on the pond. Is Hattie in one of them?

"Listen," Goldie says.

Come to think of it, my ears are picking up a lot of whooping and hollering. I do hear Hattie's voice. Angel's, too. Are they nearby?

"There!" Fetch Man says, pointing.

Food Lady shields her eyes. Muffin Lady and Tool Man do, too. "Hattie!" Food Lady calls, hopping on her toes and waving.

Muffin Lady does the same, only she cries, "Angel!"

I stand taller, my tail wagging with excitement. Because on the canoe closest to us, two short humans are waving back. It's Hattie and Angel!

Whew. My Hattie looks cheerful. And not in any danger at all.

"Our Angel is in her happy place," Patches says proudly. "She loves canoeing."

I keep my eyes on my short human as she and Angel float on the water in their puffy vests. They each hold some sort of stick that pokes into the water. It all looks perfectly safe and harmless. The other boats are not anywhere near them.

We gaze out on the water for a while, the tall humans chattering away. Until I notice another canoe gaining speed. My fur starts to prickle. Am I imagining things? Or is that other boat heading for Hattie and Angel?

I watch for a few moments to make sure. Then my hackles shoot up. In the other canoe, two short humans wear pointy, papery hats that flutter in the breeze. As they get closer to Hattie and Angel, I can hear them growling. "AARGH!" they cry, raising their sticks out of the water.

The girls must be scared the boat is going to ram into them because Angel's hand flies to her mouth. Hattie lets out a shriek. Oh no! They're scared and in trouble!

I lunge out as far as I can, my paws splashing in the water. "Hang on, Hattie!" I bark. "I'll save you!"

"FEN-way!" Fetch Man scolds, tugging me back.

"AARGH!" a boy growls again. He dips the end of his stick in the water, then sweeps it up, water spraying on Hattie and Angel.

"Hey!" they scream, ducking their heads.

"Yo-ho-ho!" one of the boys yells. His voice sounds familiar. Marcus?

Uh-oh! I knew Hattie was in danger. I take a few steps back, then spring ahead with all my might. *Splash!* The leash pulls free from Fetch Man's grip. At last!

I charge into the water. "Don't worry, Hattie! I'm coming!"

CHapteR 14

Water seeps into my fur, cold and wet.
It splashes into my eyes, my nose, my ears. But I can't
focus on any of that. I have a job to do! Nothing matters except saving My Hattie from that troublemaker
Marcus.

My paws can't grip the mushy sand anymore. They're
still scrambling, but instead of the ground, they push
against water. What a weird feeling!

Only my head is above the surface. I look around.
Water is everywhere! I spy two canoes straight ahead.
And the good news is I'm moving toward them. Some-
how I'm running. In the water!

The short humans' heads are turned in my direction.
Under their pointy, papery hats, Marcus's and the other

boy's faces look confused. The very sight of me must intimidate them because they stop splashing water on Hattie and Angel. They stop saying, "AARGH!" Their mouths are open but not making sounds.

Hattie's face is shocked. "Fenway?" she cries.

I'm coming! I'm coming! I want to bark, but as soon as I open my mouth, water splashes in. *Ew!* I spit and gag a few times. But I can't stop now. I'm almost there! I will my legs to keep pushing forward.

"FEN-way!" Hattie screams. The canoe pivots and starts heading toward me. Angel pushes her stick into the water. Hattie reaches hers out toward me. "FEN-way! FEN-way!" she keeps yelling.

The more I cough, the more I hear "FEN-way! FEN-way!" Dogs barking, too. Why is everybody suddenly calling my name? Or is the water playing tricks on my ears?

I move my legs harder and faster. Whew! I'm getting tired, but I can't slow down. I'm not far from Hattie. Thank goodness I broke away from Fetch Man in the nick of time. Hattie looks upset. Clearly, she needs me!

She leans over the side of the canoe, thrusting that stick farther and farther. I can almost reach it.

I muster what energy I have left and heave myself onto the wide part of the stick. Right then, a bunch of things happen at once.

Somebody screams, "Hattie!"

The piercing sound comes quicker and more urgent than before—*Tweet-tweet-tweeeeeet!*

Thwoosh! My head plunges under the water.

A loud *splash*, then a strong surge of water pushes me farther down. Painful water rushes up my nostrils. Bubbles tickle my whiskers. A leg kicks me.

In the next instant, I feel hands around my body. I shoot upward, breaking the water's surface. Gagging and spitting, I struggle to take in cool, fresh air. My whole face hurts. The bright sun shining on the water nearly blinds me. I shake my head.

When my eyes refocus, I see Hattie's head bobbing next to me. Her hair is wet and matted. Drops of water cling to her eyebrows, her eyelashes. She clutches me under one arm, the other paddling in the water.

I cough and cough, shaking my head some more. Owwww, does it ever ache! Who knew that water was so painful?

The canoe glides up beside us, graceful as a duck. Angel leans over, her face concerned. "You okay?" she asks.

Before Hattie can answer, the other canoe starts to head off in the opposite direction. I hear, "AARGH!" followed by fits of laughter. Obviously, I frightened them away. But what's so funny?

Grabbing me tight, Hattie kicks her legs, and we

push through the water away from the canoe. Did my heroics convince her to come back to shore?

Probably! Because we're almost there. Everyone looks worried and agitated but glad to see us. Even Goldie and Patches.

In the shallow water, Hattie gets to her feet and walks the rest of the way. She carries me to the sand, my leash hanging, dripping. She's soaked. So am I. I'm dying to shake myself off, but that'll have to wait. Saving her is way more important than my comfort.

Fetch Man and Food Lady rush over, nearly out of breath, even though they only run a couple of steps. "Oh my!" Food Lady cries.

Fetch Man takes me from Hattie and sets me in the grass. "FEN-way," he scolds, shaking a finger at me.

What's his problem? Isn't he happy that I saved Hattie? I look away and give myself a good shake. Water sprays all over him, and he jumps back, frowning.

Is he upset that I got hurt? I was only doing my duty. I shiver. Hey, when did the air get so cold?

As we hang out on the shore, you'd think everybody would be congratulating me. Hattie's arms wrapped around her chest, she leans into Food Lady, who keeps patting her sopping wet hair. She smells fishy and angry and something else. Embarrassed? Marcus must've really upset her. Still, you'd think she'd be relieved. Not to mention grateful that I rescued her from that bully.

She must still be in shock because she hasn't even thanked me.

"You can't help it, Fenway," Patches says in a soothing voice. "When it comes to Hattie, you tend to go a little overboard."

"Now that you mention it," Goldie says. "You have done some nutty things in the name of protecting your short human."

I thrust out my chest, my wet tail high and proud. "Just doing my job."

Goldie stares at me for a moment, like she's thinking. Then she says, "Have you ever thought you might go too far sometimes?"

"Now, Goldie," Patches says. "Fenway's intentions are good."

Before I can ask what that means, Angel comes charging over. She looks as flustered as everyone else. After a few rushed words and pats on the back, we all head to the path in the pine trees.

The walk back to the clearing is quiet. Being unappreciated by my humans is one thing. But by my friends? What's up with that? I thought we came to the woods to make friends, not lose them.

When we get back, the ladies follow Tool Man and Muffin Lady over to their campsite by the big oak tree. I give myself another shake, but it doesn't make me feel better.

And speaking of not feeling better, Hattie squats down in front of me. She's traded the puffy vest for a big plush towel. A wet lock of hair is matted against her forehead. "FEN-way," she scolds, wagging a finger. I don't know what she says after that, but she keeps on using that "you're in trouble" voice.

My tail droops and I take a step back, my heart breaking into hundreds of little pieces. Why is Hattie mad? What did I do? I was only trying to save her. Who knows what would've happened if I hadn't been there?

Fetch Man comes at me with another plush towel. He smells mad, too. Normally, I love cozy towel rubs, especially from Hattie. But the whole time Fetch Man rubs me down, he talks to me in a scolding voice. Talk about taking the fun out of something.

And worse, when he's done, he ties my leash around the bench. I look around the clearing. Hattie disappears inside the tent. Except for the buzzing of insects, it's strangely silent. Apparently, Coco and her humans aren't back from hiking in the woods. Since the pine tree June usually sits under is empty, I'm guessing she's inside her tent with Waddling Lady.

Goldie and Patches are already curled up napping. Angel sits on the bench, changing her shoes. Tool Man and Muffin Lady drink from paper cups.

Sudden rustling sounds—no, footsteps and jingling dog tags—pull my attention to the trees. Hammock Man and Lucky trot into the clearing. They're both breathing hard. Lucky's tongue lolls to the side. Hammock Man takes off his bandanna and mops his brow with it.

I sink to the ground, my ears wilted along with my spirits. I give my paw a lick, even though that's not the part of me that hurts. I'm about to close my eyes and try to sleep off my sadness when Angel lets out a wail.

Chapter 15

"What the—?" Angel cries.

I leap to my feet. Angel's standing near the Fire Space on the far side of their boxy tent, holding out a bag and showing it to Tool Man. I'm too far away to investigate, but even from here I pick up smoky, meaty aromas. A strong, musky odor, too. Is that the bag of bacon from this morning?

It's ripped and torn. Uh-oh. What happened?

Muffin Lady rushes over. She looks concerned. So does Tool Man.

The ladies trot toward me, and I whip around. "Oh my!" Patches cries. "Somebody got into that bacon!"

"This is what happens when our Angel leaves food out," Goldie scowls.

I can't believe my ears. Or my eyes. The ladies sound like Coco. And they're heading in the wrong direction. "Aren't you going to sniff for clues?" I say. Maybe the strong, musky odor I picked up was coming from somewhere else.

"Fenway," Patches says gently. "What's done is done."

"Yeah, but don't you want to know who did it? Whoever it was could come back!"

"Not if the food's put away," Goldie says. Now she really sounds like Coco!

Patches gives me a gentle nuzzle. "Try not to worry, Fenway. Not everything is a dangerous threat."

How can she say that? We're in the middle of the woods!

Angel and Tool Man and Muffin Lady all talk at once. Fetch Man strolls over. "Oh no," he says, shaking his head.

Hattie's right behind him. She's wearing different clothes, but her hair is tussled and damp. "Please untie me, Hattie," I bark, straining on the leash. "I need to go over there and investigate."

She turns back, and my tail wags with hope. Until I notice one eyebrow's raised. "Fenway, stay," she says in a growly voice before catching up to Fetch Man.

Coco must've been watching as her humans returned from hiking, because she charges up at that very moment. "When will you learn to mind your own business, *Fenway*?" Her voice is mean and ominous.

I leap back. What does she know? Protecting Hattie *is* my business. Even if Hattie won't let me. "You don't know what you're yapping about," I say to Coco.

"I know what I saw," she says. "Even your short human doesn't want you sniffing all over. That's why you're on that leash while the rest of us aren't." Thrusting out her chest, she spins around and swaggers off.

My tail droops. What a show-off. I'm vaguely aware of humans and dogs making noise and moving around the campsite, but I can't focus on anything. Except what just happened.

Coco was gone. Could Lucky have done it? He seemed guilty before. Maybe he stole that bacon.

But even if I can't sniff that package as much as I'd like, I don't know if Lucky had the chance to get at it. Smelling is believing. I wish I could be sure.

Across the clearing—*vwoop!*—a tent zipper opens. Hammock Man comes out, minus the bandanna, Lucky bounding after him, full of playful energy. Not acting suspicious at all.

Or is he? Suddenly, he reverses direction and hurries back to the tent. I watch his tail thump heavily as

June comes out, her arms wrapped around a book. She strides over to her usual pine tree and plops down. He follows her over and curls up at her feet.

I keep focused on him. What if he goes straight for one of the Food Boxes the moment I glance away? I have to know if there's any way he was the thief.

I study June for clues, but she only has eyes for that open book in her lap. Other than turning the pages every now and then, she is perfectly still.

After a while, Hattie strolls over to her. Her hair is still damp, but it's much neater than it was before. She drops down beside June, smiling and pointing at the book.

At first, I think she and June are going to chatter again or maybe put paint on their cheeks. But even from here, I can see June's face scrunch up, her eyes narrowing. She gets to her feet and looks down at Hattie. Her long braid falls over her shoulder.

Lucky's eyes gaze up at June, but the rest of him doesn't move.

Hattie's face is surprised. "What?" I hear her say. She swats at a fly.

June reaches into her pocket. She holds out her closed fist. When she opens her hand, a ball of crumpled paper falls out and floats to the ground. June folds her arms across her chest. She's not loud, but I can tell she is mad. Her voice sounds sad and hurt.

Hattie is quiet, her expression blank. Her eyes start to shine.

June's eyes start shining, too. She sniffs a few times. She plops back down and begins patting Lucky like she just remembered he was there. She rests her head against his back and wipes her nose.

Clearly, the short humans are both upset by that rumpled paper. But why? It seems pretty harmless to me.

Hattie snatches the crumpled ball and turns away, like she can't bear to look at June. She starts to rush off toward our campsite.

Just then, I hear footsteps and noisy chatter arriving from the dirt road. Marcus storms in with another boy. They're both wearing those pointy, papery hats, growling "AARGH!" and singing "Yo-ho-ho!"

Hattie swerves out of their path, cowering like she's hoping they won't notice her. Her gaze is fixed on the ground. Apparently, she can't bear to look at them, either. She slinks quickly toward the domed tent as if she can't wait to escape.

They point and snicker. I hear "AARGH!" a few more times and "land-lub-ber!" followed by more laughing.

As Hattie gets closer to me, I see wet tears streaming down her face. She unzips the tent and disappears inside.

Big feet come up to the bench. Tool Man's voice is chattering with Fetch Man. I creep out for a peek.

They're studying the ripped package of bacon—specifically the bite marks. Which are awfully tiny.

I have a terrible feeling about whose teeth did the damage. I shoot a look at Lucky, sprawled out under the tree across the clearing. He opens his mouth for a yawn. A big, wide yawn.

His teeth are huge.

My fur bristles. There's no way he bit into that bacon.

And if he didn't do it, and Coco didn't do it, my worst nightmare has come true!

CHapter 16

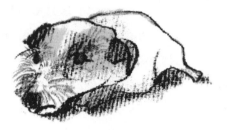

I want to melt into the ground. My body sinks, my ears flattened against my head. But I can't relax. My muscles feel as tight as a tug-of-war rope. And hard as rocks.

How did everything get so messed up? A wild animal must have snuck into our campsite—three times!—and stolen food. Hattie's obviously not safe.

I was fooling myself by suspecting Coco and Lucky. And if only I could've found a way to sniff any of the evidence, I would have realized that sooner. Now my short human is in danger, and she's anything but happy. I've failed at my two most important jobs.

Poor Hattie. Ever since June got mad and Marcus teased her, Hattie's been inside that tent all by herself.

My heart aches as I listen to her staggered breathing and sniffles.

This is not how it's supposed to be. The ladies said short humans and their families come to the woods every year. For tradition. To be with a big group of friends. Not to be alone. Or sad.

If I weren't tied to this bench, I'd race to her side and snuggle against her until she's happy again. Except I think of how she didn't appreciate that I saved her in the water, and I get the feeling that anything I do won't be enough.

I lie here doing nothing for a Long, Long Time. Food Lady sits at the table with Muffin Lady and Waddling Lady. Every now and then, one of them says, "rum-my," followed by the clattering and fluttering sound of cards. The other humans are quiet. The other dogs are either lounging or out of sight. I'm about to wonder if this horrible, lonely afternoon will ever end when out of the corner of my eye Angel appears from around a tree.

I lift my head. She's coming this way. Are things about to get better?

After chatting with Food Lady for a moment, she dashes toward the tent. "Hattie?" she calls.

My ears rise, hoping to hear my beloved Hattie's voice. But all I hear is a fly buzzing overhead.

"Hattie?" Angel calls again. Her voice is a bit more forceful this time.

I tilt my head toward the tent. Hattie's got to be in there.

I start to wonder if maybe she snuck out and somehow I didn't notice. But then I hear *vwoop!* and my hopes soar. Hattie's coming out!

Or maybe not. Angel hesitates for a second, then steps inside the tent. *Rizzzzz!* She closes the zipper behind her. "Hey," she says.

As the short humans chat in low voices, I strain to listen. It sounds like Angel is asking Hattie some questions. Or trying to coax her into something.

Hattie mutters, her tone gloomy and doubtful. She must not want to go along. I pick up "the crew" a couple of times.

"Come on." Angel almost sounds like she's begging.

Hattie goes quiet. I begin to think she's through with chatting, but then she speaks in an even gloomier voice. I catch her say, "Marcus" and "no way."

But Angel doesn't sound like she's giving up. Now she's pleading.

I'm not sure what's going on, except I can tell that Hattie is not feeling better. I'm actually afraid she might be worse.

"No-big-deel," Angel keeps saying. And, "Come on."

143

Hattie goes silent again. Then I hear her murmuring, followed by *vwooop!*

My tail lifts hopefully. Is she finally coming back?

Angel pops out of the tent. Without Hattie.

Rizzzzz! The zipper zips shut, and Angel heads across the clearing. I watch the back of her dark hair until she disappears through the pine trees.

I slump back on the ground. If Angel can't coax Hattie out, she must really want to be alone.

"Rum-my," Food Lady says. I wait for the sounds of clattering and fluttering cards, but this time the tall humans speak in hushed tones. I catch "Hattie" and "friends" once or twice and then "new-skool." They sound concerned.

I know how they feel. I wish there were something I could do to help my short human. I rest my head on my brown paw. I can't be with her. I can't see her. I can barely smell her.

All I can do is listen.

Too bad the tent is completely quiet. Or is it?

Ignoring the tall humans, the cawing birds, and the rustle of the breeze in the branches, I pay attention as hard as I can for sounds of Hattie. My ears in total focus, at last I pick up *swooosh-thsssss-thsssss.*

Is that a pencil on paper? Is Hattie drawing?

I remember last night—the flashlight, the notebook,

the horse's head, the pole coming out of it. I concentrate on the sounds. *Swooosh-thsssss-thsssss.* I let out a sigh. It's actually pretty relaxing. Is that what Hattie's doing? Is she relaxing?

I sigh again, picturing her lying on her belly, propped up on her elbows. Her hand gripping a pencil, moving across a pad of paper.

Just when I start to get hopeful again, the sounds change. They're suddenly louder, sharper, faster.

Thwusss-thwuss-thwuss. R-r-r-r-ip! R-r-r-r-ip!

Uh-oh. I don't need to smell her to know she's mad and frustrated again. I wait for a moment, my hopes smashed to bits, then all goes silent again.

I should've known.

The tall humans must hear it, too, because they stop murmuring. Food Lady gets up from the table and walks over to the tent. She leans in. "Hattie?"

When Hattie doesn't answer—*vwooop!*—the zipper opens, and Food Lady ducks inside.

"Hattie," I hear her say in a low tone.

I raise my head, my ears cocked and listening.

"Well," Hattie starts. She speaks quickly, her voice gaining steam as she goes on. I can't tell what she's talking about, but I catch snippets—"the crew," "Marcus," "Angel," and then finally, "June" and "yoon-ih-corns." Then I hear the sounds of ripping paper again.

"Oh, bay-bee," Food Lady says in a comforting voice.

Hattie chatters some more. This time the only name I hear is "June." The longer she talks, the stronger her voice gets. Hattie sounds less sad and more sure. Determined.

My tail perks up. Is this good news? Is Hattie beginning to feel better?

Just then, I hear a snap! Like a human's foot crunching on a twig. Fetch Man strides into the campsite. Hot Dog Man is right behind him, a small dog's face peeking over his shoulder. I don't need to smell her to know it's Coco riding in the backpack again.

She must spot me, too, because she starts glowering.

My fur bristles, and I slink back under the bench. Is this how things are going to be from now on? Coco's in charge, and we all have to do things her way? She wouldn't stand up to the thieves who raided her family's Food Box or Marcus's backpack, and now the ladies aren't bothering to guard their family's food, either. It's like they're inviting a wild animal to take over our campsite!

All our humans are in danger. And nobody cares except me.

I make up my mind then and there. Maybe the rest of them are fine going along with Coco, but that doesn't mean I have to.

Chapter 17

Later, when mouthwatering chicken is sizzling on the Fire Space and Marcus and Angel are playing chase around the campsite, Hattie's still in the tent by herself. I can hear her scribbling away, probably in that notebook again. Ever since we came back from the pond, it seems to be the only thing she's really interested in. Every *thwusss* stabs at my heart. I'm supposed to be in there with her, listening to the comm-ix story. Not tied up outside by myself.

Hot Dog Man sets lots of plates on the table while Swirly-Arm Lady piles chicken high on a platter. The other humans start making their way over, and who can blame them? Barbecued chicken is irresistible.

My tongue starts dripping. That chicken won't help

me figure out what to do or make Hattie happy, but it sure couldn't hurt.

Marcus catches up to Angel and lets out a loud "Whoop!" Laughing, they bound up to the table, where the human families are already seated. Except for one.

Fetch Man strolls over to the tent. "Hattie?" he calls.

Hattie stops scribbling, but I don't hear her voice. Or the zipper opening up. Isn't she coming out to eat supper?

Food Lady joins Fetch Man, her face concerned. "Let-er-bee," she says to him in a soft voice.

I don't know what that means, but Fetch Man shrugs and puts his arm around her. They head toward the next table and the food. Without Hattie.

Uh-oh. My hackles bristle. This is all kinds of wrong. How can Hattie miss out on supper? She loves barbecued chicken!

The others greet Fetch Man and Food Lady with questioning looks. "Hattie?" I hear one of the tall humans ask. Clearly, everybody is wondering why she's the only one not eating. Well, the only human, that is.

Fetch Man and Food Lady exchange a quick glance, then slide into their seats. Whatever Fetch Man says seems to satisfy the rest of them because they dig in to the food as if somebody just not eating happens all the time.

I turn toward the tent, my heart aching. Poor Hattie! I sure wouldn't want to miss out on supper.

I lower my head, trying to ignore my own rumbling tummy. If Hattie's not here, that means no chicken scraps for me. I certainly wouldn't steal it, unlike some creatures.

It's ridiculous to think that wild animals can invade our campsite anytime they want. Coco and the other dogs act like it's no big deal. I have to take matters into my own paws.

As the tall humans clean the table, I watch June wander across the clearing and plop down under that same pine tree. She picks up her book and flips it open. I remember what the ladies said when we first got here. *She's not in the crew anymore. That must be why she's sitting by herself.*

Shouts and squeals bring my attention back toward the garbage bin. Marcus and Angel are playing chase again. They weave in and out of the tables and tents, laughing. I hear a mysterious word, "bonn-fire," a few times. Eventually, Angel slows to a stop not far from me. She hunches over, her hands on her knees, smiling and panting. I hear her say, "Hattie."

Marcus scowls. "Whatever," he mutters.

Angel lopes over to the tent. "Hattie?" she calls, leaning into the zipper. I hear "the crew" and "bonn-fire?"

I tilt my head in her direction. I can't tell if Hattie mumbles a response, or if that's just the breeze rustling a couple of fallen leaves.

Angel pauses. Waiting? But Hattie doesn't come out. She must give up, because after a moment or two, she rushes back over to Marcus. They head out through the trees, chanting, "Bonn-fire! Bonn-fire!"

Fetch Man and Food Lady stroll back to our campsite. My tail comes to life. Because Food Lady grabs my bowl. I know what's coming next!

"Hooray! Hooray!" I bark, leaping and twirling. "It's sup-sup-suppertime! The very best time of the day!"

Sure enough, the familiar bag crinkles open. Fetch Man unleashes me as meaty, crunchy morsels clatter into the dish.

Ordinarily, nothing can distract me from suppertime. But the sound of the zipper opening—*vwoop!*—makes my heart soar. Hattie is coming!

I romp over to the tent. Hattie's head of short hair appears, then the rest of her, the notebook tucked under her arm. *Rizzzzz!* The zipper closes.

"Hattie! Hattie!" I bark, pawing her legs. "I missed you so much."

"Shhh, Fenway," she murmurs. She barely looks at me. She must be very focused. And in a hurry?

I hardly notice Food Lady place my bowl on the ground. I follow Hattie across the clearing toward June. Her face bright and hopeful, she sinks down beside June. "Uh-bowt—um," Hattie says, fidgeting.

June keeps her gaze on the book while Hattie keeps talking, then looks up, her face surprised.

Hattie hangs her head. "Sorry."

June looks serious. "It's okay," she says.

What's that about?

"Fenn-waay," Food Lady sings, gesturing toward my dish. As if my roaring belly could let me forget about supper!

I race back to my bowl of delicious kibble. It smells savory and meaty like always. I'm so hungry! I'm about to plunge my snout in and devour it—

But right then, I get an idea. The Best Idea Ever!

@Hapter 18

I stick my snout inside the bowl and root around. The kibble rattles against the sides, same as always. *Mmmmm!* It sounds as yummy as it tastes!

After devouring half the kibble, I sneak a peek at my humans. Food Lady's at the table, pouring a drink from the big thermos. Fetch Man is at the next campsite over, chatting with Hot Dog Man beside the garbage bin. Swirly-Arm Lady wipes the table. Coco is nowhere to be seen. I'd bet my best bone she's in the tent, curled up on her squishy bed.

I sniff the smoky remnants of that barbecued chicken in the air. My tummy rumbles. My tongue drips. But I can't keep eating or my plan won't work.

I spy Hattie across the clearing under the pine tree with June. Her notebook open, she's pointing at the pages. June stares, eyebrows arched like she's watching her dog do a trick. The two short humans are clearly occupied. No way are they noticing me.

Nobody is.

Hammock Man and Waddling Lady are sitting across from Tool Man and Muffin Lady at their table. They are drinking from metal cups and chattering away. The ladies, their bowls probably empty and licked, are lounging at their tall humans' feet. Lucky's in the middle of the clearing chasing his tail.

The sun is so low in the sky, I can't see it over the treetops. Stripe-y shadows line the ground at the edge of the woods. A single cricket is chirping.

My tummy still hungry, I turn my head from my dish. I remind myself why I'm doing this—I have to show that thief who he's up against. And make sure he knows he can never come back here. Ever.

And I have to move fast.

I hustle over to the next campsite, past Goldie and Patches's car, past their tent. They're still sprawled out beside the wooden table where their tall humans are chatting with Hammock Man and Waddling Lady. "Ladies!" I holler.

"Not now, Fenway," Goldie says without moving.

Patches looks up. "Don't mind her," she says. "What is it?"

I give myself a shake. This might be tougher than I thought. "Um, so I hate to interrupt your important after-supper lounging," I start. "But I need you. Like right now."

Patches pushes onto her paws, her tail wagging. "We're always ready to help a friend, aren't we, Goldie?"

Goldie rolls onto her side. "Well, that's not exactly what I would say. But it'd better be good because I just found the perfect position."

"Oh, this will be worth it." I sure hope so, anyway. "And there's no time to lose, so we've got to hurry."

Patches noses Goldie in the bum. "You heard Fenway," she says. "Let's get going."

I lead the ladies over to my supper dish. Another minute or so, and Food Lady will be back to take my bowl. After one more check to make sure there isn't anybody watching, I chomp the edge of the dish. Calm as can be, I walk alongside the bench toward the cool, empty Fire Space until I'm mere pawsteps from the woods.

The ladies follow me past the big oak tree by the path that leads to the Dog Park. We creep along the edge of the woods toward the back of my humans' campsite. A slightly musky odor lingers nearby. Yikes!

The forest is already getting dark, but it's clearly not sleepy. Leaves flutter, branches creak. Insects trill, cheep, and beat. It's practically alive.

Sniff . . . sniff . . .

Pine. Oak. Decaying leaves.

Soil. Moss. Fungus of all kinds.

Birds. Rodents. Wild animals I can't identify.

Shivering with courage, I set the bowl on the ground. One swipe and it's on its side, kibble spilling onto the ground. Before I can talk myself out of it, I kick pine needles over the yummy food.

"Fenway!" the ladies mutter at once.

After shushing them, I ask them to keep an eye on that spot until I get back.

I race back to the table with my dish and heave a sigh of relief. Food Lady is rummaging through a bag. She probably didn't even miss me.

I wait until Food Lady comes for the empty bowl before setting the rest of the plan into motion. No point in making her suspicious.

"Good boy, Fenway," she says, patting my head as usual.

"Good supper, Food Lady," I bark, licking her hand as usual. Her fingers taste like barbecue sauce.

I keep my eyes on her as she puts the dish away and heads over to Swirly-Arm Lady. When I'm sure her attention is elsewhere, I get back to work.

As casual as can be, I follow Food Lady. I trot past

the garbage bin, past Fetch Man and Hot Dog Man, past the wooden table where Food Lady sits down.

Every hair on my back bristling, I push on to the boxy tent. As I get closer, I notice the zipper's not zipped all the way. I poke my snout, then my whole head inside. "Coco! Oh, Co-co!" I call. "It's me, Fenway!"

Her fluffy ears rise up from the puffy dog bed. "What do you want, *Fenway*?"

"Not much," I say, steadying my voice. "Just taking a stroll."

"And you decided to stop by and say hello?" she growls. "What gave you the idea that I'd care?"

I try to shake off her nastiness. "Um, you probably have better things to do, Coco. But I wanted you to know that there's, uh, something you're going to want to see behind our Fire Space."

She snorts. "Something I can't resist? Unless it's a T-bone steak, you're wasting your time."

Aha! "Whoa, that's actually what it is—a T-bone steak!"

"Do you expect me to believe there's a T-bone steak up for grabs and you're letting me have it?" Coco says with a snarl. "I saw you scarf down that hot dog the first night we were here."

"I know I haven't been respectful of your leadership

in the past, Coco," I say, bowing my head. "But I'm try-ing to make peace."

"Hmmph!" I hear her say. And then, "Not that I be-lieve you, but where did you say this T-bone steak was again?"

I keep my gaze down. "By my human's Fire Space. On the edge of the woods. Anyway, I have to get back to my stroll. See you around."

She growls. "Don't count on it."

That dog is totally on the hook! I back out and sprint in the direction of our campsite. I'm halfway there when Lucky bounds up beside me. "Oh, hey, Fenway!" he says. "What's going on?" His muzzle is filthy, like he's been playing in dirt.

My tail shoots up. "Nothing as exciting as digging a hole!" I cry. "You probably want to get back to that. Bye!"

Lucky's eyes widen. "I'd rather hang out with you," he says, his tongue hanging low and spraying slobber. "Ohmygosh, I found an old tennis ball! We could play keep-away!!!"

I dart in front of him. "Maybe later, Lucky! I gotta go!" I zip around the far side of our tent and sprint to-ward the Fire Space, where the ladies are waiting.

I sure hope I'm not too late for the festivities.

When I reach them, they exchange looks but don't

say anything. The woods are darker than they were even a few minutes ago. Insects are whirring. Leaves are rustling. Twigs are crunching and snapping. Is it my imagination, or are there more noises tonight?

I lead the ladies behind the tent. "Just wait," I say in a low voice.

"What are we doing?" Goldie mutters.

"Isn't it obvious?" Patches murmurs. "We're helping a friend."

Good old Patches. I'd thank her, but hopefully there will be time for that later. Because through the trees, through the brush, I spy little pricks of light glowing. Moving. Like eyes!

Yowza! Are they headed this way?

CHapteR 19

Yikes! My tail droops, my fur rises, and all I want to do is get out of here! But I have to stay and finish the job. There's too much at stake!

Quietly, cautiously, me and the ladies peer around the side of our tent. Toward the Fire Space.

Through the dim light, I spy Coco coming around the far side of our car. And somebody else is bolting around the other side—Lucky!

"What're they doing here?" Goldie mutters.

I want to say they're supposed to be my witnesses, but they're too early. Instead I just nudge Goldie silent.

Snout to the ground, Coco is so focused on sniffing the pine needles, she doesn't seem to notice Lucky until the last second.

"Hey, Coco!" he cries, bowing low on his front legs. "What's going on?"

My fur stands on end. I want to race over there and tell him to be quiet, but the rustling, snapping sounds in the woods are growing louder. And closer. I try to convince myself not to look, but I can't help it.

I turn toward the thick, dark woods, my paws trembling and shaking. Because up ahead, two pricks of light come shooting out from the brush! Double yikes! Those eyes can't possibly see us behind the tent, can they?

I lean into Goldie, cowering and shivering. "What the—?" she mutters.

"Look!" Patches murmurs.

Eyes are glowing through a black mask. On a furry face with pointy ears. Attached to a fat body with four thin legs and a bushy tail. And a mouth with scary, sharp fangs!

Chit-chit-cheeeeet! He sounds almost like a bird. But this guy is definitely not a bird! He smells strong and musky.

I huddle against Goldie, watching in horror as a second wild animal, exactly the same, follows the first one out of the woods. Triple yikes! It's an invasion! I was ready for one, not two!

They're each about my height but way wider around. They're prowling like cats. Big, chubby cats! With horrifying, fiery eyes!

The animals toddle toward our Fire Space, zeroing in on the bait like they've done this a hundred times. One sweeps the pine needles while the other rolls the kibble on the ground with his tiny paw. The first one stretches up on his haunches, stuffing his mouth. The second one does, too.

I want to charge right out and stop them, but it's not time. Coco's so distracted with Lucky, she hasn't even noticed them yet. Also, my shaking paws probably wouldn't listen!

"Well, would you look at that," Patches murmurs. "Real, live raccoons!"

"I've heard raccoons are ugly, but these guys are worse than I imagined," Goldie says.

I'm about to say they smell worse, too, when a couple of yelps—one tiny and one big—draw my attention to a spot near the car.

Coco and Lucky are frozen in place, ears sunk, tails wilted. Two more raccoons are right behind them! They must've just come out from behind the car and into the thick of the action. Those dogs are cornered! This was not part of the plan.

The first two raccoons swivel toward Coco and Lucky. Rearing up on their hind legs, their front paws stretch out. Talk about menacing!

"Hiiiiiisssss! Hiiiiiisssss! Hiiiiiisssss!" they spit.

Yikes for the fourth time!

"Hiiiiiisssss! Hiiiiiisssss! Hiiiiiisssss!" the raccoons spit again. The claws on their front paws are the very definition of threatening.

Coco looks like she's half her usual size. Lucky slinks back, whimpering. They're surrounded by angry raccoons. And clearly terrified.

They're not the only ones! I'm supposed to do something, except my legs refuse to move. If you don't count shaking. This plan is going worse than I could have imagined.

I want to run and hide. But right then, I hear a familiar voice calling. "Fenway? Fenway?"

Hattie?! What's she doing here? She's supposed to be under the pine tree on the other side of the clearing.

I turn in time to see her rushing past the wooden table, her face worried. Oh no! She's headed straight for those horrible raccoons! My beloved short human!

Before I realize what I'm doing, I blast out from behind the tent. My hackles are raised. My teeth are bared. "Beat it, you crooks!" I bark, snarling my fiercest snarl. "Stay away from My Hattie!"

164

The first two raccoons whip around, their mouths open, their fangs glistening in the dim light. "Screeeeech! Screeeeech!"

I lunge at them but stop mere steps away. I can smell their disgusting breath. "You heard me!" I bark. "Scram! Before it's too late!"

The raccoons behind Coco and Lucky whip around and take off into the woods. Their stripe-y, bushy tails are the last things I see as they disappear into the brush.

I focus back on the two raccoons in front of me, growling and baring my teeth. "Go ahead, get out of here!" I bark. "I mean business!"

"Hiiiissssss-hiiiissssss! Screeeeech!" The crooks keep up the fight, their eyes glaring and determined. As if they have a chance!

"Fenway!" Hattie arrives, out of breath, wielding a flashlight. Suddenly, a swath of bright light shines on the raccoons.

Whoa! Those raccoons look even scarier all lit up! But I can't give up now. "Don't come near her!" I bark. "Or else!"

And just like that, with a series of squeaks and squeals, they turn tail. Next thing I know, they're dashing off to the woods to join the others.

"Fenway!" Hattie cries, swooping me into her arms. She snuggles me tight. I can feel her chest thumping.

Patches races over to Coco and Lucky. Goldie's right behind her. "What a fright!" Patches cries. "Are you two okay?"

Goldie licks Lucky's ear. "If I hadn't seen it, I wouldn't believe it!"

Coco is silent as Patches checks her out. "You don't seem hurt," Patches says. "Physically, anyway." Then she turns around. "Fenway, you're a hero!"

Hattie sets me down and showers my neck with kisses. What can I say? My short human appreciates me. As soon as she straightens, we hear sharp snaps and scuffling sounds in the woods, followed by loud shrieks. Human shrieks.

We all turn. Somebody's in those woods. With the scary raccoons!

"Oh my!" Patches cries. "Was that our precious Angel?"

Goldie looks horrified. "Maybe it was your imagination?"

I cock my head and listen. It does sound like Angel's voice among those shrieks.

Hattie must hear her, too. Because she hurries to the edge of the woods. Where it's totally not safe. "Angel?! Angel?!" she yells, her arms flailing frantically.

Oh no! Just when I thought we were out of danger. "Hold on, Hattie!" I bark, charging up to her side. "I've got this!"

"Fenway, are you sure you—" Patches's voice trails off as I plunge through the trees.

I scamper through prickly brush, over a fallen branch, and around a rotting tree trunk. The shrieks are louder. Nearer.

The woods are dark and thick. The strong, musky odors are terrifying. I see specks of glowing light in the distance. Eyes? Or something else?

I hear more rustling and snapping sounds. "Help! Help!" somebody screams. The voice sounds familiar. It's coming closer. Whoever it is smells like grape jelly. And dirt.

I dive under a downed branch, shoot through thorny bushes, and leap over a rock. "I'm warning you for the last time, raccoons! Stay away!"

"Hiiiissssss-hiiiissssss! Screeeeech!"

Crash! Crackle! Snap! Leaves crunch. Brush sways. Those terrified raccoons are bolting out of here as fast as they can!

"Fenway?" Angel's voice calls.

I turn as she comes rushing toward me, her face overjoyed, her arms outstretched. She squats down, and I leap at her knee. "Hooray!" I bark, licking her cheek. She tastes like burnt marshmallows. She's clearly grateful that I saved her from the vicious raccoons.

Marcus comes racing up with a flashlight. His eyes

are huge. His cheeks are huffing and puffing. He's obviously scared. Other short humans come trudging after him. They're all shouting in panicked voices.

"Whoa!" one of them shrieks.

"Didya see them?" shouts another.

Marcus and the others follow me and Angel out of the woods. We reach the edge of the campsite and nearly run smack into Hattie and Fetch Man.

"Fenway!" Hattie cries.

The ladies race up to us. "Oh, thank goodness our precious Angel is saved!" Patches shouts as Angel sets me down. Hattie squats beside me, patting my back.

Goldie nuzzles Angel's face and gets her ears scratched in return.

Out of nowhere, June comes rushing up to Lucky, who's still lying on the ground, whimpering. "Aw, poor Lucky," she soothes, rubbing his head. He noses her cheek.

Marcus bends over, his hands on his knees. He's obviously tired. And relieved. A group of other short humans gathers at his side. When one pats Marcus on the shoulder, his head snaps up, startled.

Hattie lays her head on mine, but her eyes are looking at Marcus. "Good boy, Fenway," she says in a much louder tone than necessary.

Marcus and the other short humans turn to me.

"Fenway?" one of them cries. "Puppy?" another says in a surprised voice. It's obviously dawned on them who scared off those villains and saved the day.

Next thing I know, I'm surrounded. Hands are petting me and rubbing my neck and stroking my ears. "Aw, shucks, everybody," I bark. "I was just doing my job."

As Marcus and the short humans go off in all directions, the ladies come up to me. Goldie cocks her head. "Like I said, when it comes to Hattie, you do tend to go a little overboard."

"Not only did you scare away those raccoons," Patches says, "but you showed everyone who stole the humans' food!"

"It wasn't much of a surprise," Goldie says. "The whole operation smacked of raccoons from the beginning."

I thrust out my chest. "I would've run them off sooner if somebody had let me near the evidence . . ."

"Well, thanks to you, Fenway, those mischief makers won't be back anytime soon," Patches says.

"Those wild animals wouldn't dare show their faces—or masks—as long as I'm around." I glance over at Lucky, sighing contentedly in June's arms. Then I see Coco, wandering back to the campsite. Alone.

CHAPTER 20

Late at night, me and Hattie are zipped up in the padded blankets. I nestle against her cheek, her short hair tickling my nose. Me and my beloved short human are together, safe, and cozy. Sighing with happiness, I close my eyes and drift off to sleep.

And suddenly, voices are chattering. "Help! Help!"

Uh-oh! Somebody's in trouble! I spring up and head outside, my fur standing on end. "Don't worry, whoever you are!" I bark, gazing around. "I'll save you!"

Even though it's totally dark, I can tell the campsite is empty. No tall humans. No short humans. No dogs. Where did everybody go?

I raise my snout and sniff the air for clues. But there's

nothing. Not even a bit of smoky bacon. And no tasty hot dogs, either.

Hey, wait a minute. Where's all the food?

I race over to our Food Box, my eyes widening in horror. It's totally empty!

I sprint over to the ladies' Food Box. Same thing!

Coco's Food Box, Lucky's Food Box. Not one speck of food anywhere! Oh no! What happened?

"Help! Help!" Those voices again! Where are they coming from?

"Hold on!" I bark. "The hero is coming!" I search the whole campsite, but I can't find anybody or anything. There's only one thing left to do—explore the woods.

As soon as I charge into the brush, the voices are louder. "Help! Help!" More of them. "Help! Help! Help! Help!"

My head swivels. A pair of dots glows up ahead. A long way ahead. "Fenway, help!" a voice calls. I start to bound down the path.

"Over here, Fenway!" another voice calls. I pull to a stop. Two more eyes shine down from the way-up-high treetops. How am I supposed to get up there?

"This way, Fenway! I need you!" cry other voices far off in the distance. "Come quick, Fenway!" "Hurry, Fenway!"

"Help! Help! Help!"

I dart one way, then the other. I don't want to be in charge. I only want some friends! I just want to—!

"Fenway?" I hear Hattie's voice. I feel her fingers rubbing my neck.

Morning light seeps into the tent. I gaze into my short human's sleepy eyes. I crawl into Hattie's arms, and she hugs me tight. Why am I panting?

Hattie grabs the nearest shirt and shorts and pulls them on. She tucks her notebook and some pencils under her arm. Running her fingers through her short hair, she unzips the door—*vwoop!*—and we step into the scents of fresh air mingled with smoke, coffee, and sweet sausage.

Mmmmm!

Fetch Man and Food Lady hover over the wooden table. Food Lady offers Hattie a cup of juice, but she shakes her head. She smells determined. And she walks with purpose, like she's on a mission.

I follow Hattie across the clearing to the tall pine tree. June's seated on the bench, munching a plate of scrambled eggs while Waddling Lady paints her face.

"Hey," Hattie says, smiling. She slides onto the bench beside June.

When June's cheek is full of stripe-y curves, she turns to show Hattie. "Cool-rain-boh," Hattie says, her voice full of admiration.

"Thanks," June says in a small voice.

Waddling Lady points her paintbrush at Hattie. "Yoo-too?" she asks.

Hattie nods, her face busting into a grin. When Waddling Lady is finished, Hattie's cheek has a pair of delicate-looking wings on it.

"Cool-fair-ee," June says. She and Hattie giggle.

When Waddling Lady puts the brush down, Hattie places the notebook on the table and lays it open. She hands June one of her pencils.

Whoopee! I know what's coming next.

June looks up, excited.

I paw Hattie's leg. "Don't forget me!" I bark.

Hattie lifts me onto the bench. I leap up, my front paws gripping the table. Hattie and June get busy talking and drawing and making marks on the pages. Lines and curves, too. Pretty soon, the paper is covered with images and boxes. They're both focused but also full of energy.

When they're finished, June grins.

Hattie's grin is even wider. If it makes her this happy, I guess it's okay that she shared our special comm-ix with somebody else.

After breakfast, Hattie clips my leash and leads me to the big oak tree. Hooray! Hooray! We're going to the Dog Park! June and Lucky are waiting for us on the path.

"Ohmygosh! Ohmygosh!" Lucky says, his tail swinging wildly. He pretty much repeats this over and over until we reach the maple tree and the chain-link fence. Besides me, he might be the most enthusiastic dog I know.

The Dog Park is bustling with action. Big dogs, little dogs, wide dogs, thin dogs. Apparently, everybody decided to play all at the same time. Can't argue with that!

As we rush through the gate, I spy the ladies near the front bench. After I do the bum-sniffing circle dance with them, Angel comes over and pats my head. I lick her hand. She tastes like pancakes. When she stands up, she gestures toward Hattie's face.

Hattie beams. "Like it?" she says proudly. She takes her notebook out from under her arm and plops down on the bench. She flips through the pages, showing them to Angel.

Angel peers over the notebook. "You made these?" she asks them both. She sounds impressed.

June swings her long braid over her shoulder. She watches Hattie show the rest of the notebook to Angel, her whole face grinning.

"Hey, is that Fenway?" I hear one of the dogs call.

"Did you hear about last night?" cries another. "He saved the crew from a pack of bears!"

"You mean a moose!" another dog cries.

"That Fenway is one tough dog!" a couple of others say.

"Looks like you're the big dog now," Goldie says in a teasing voice.

"You've earned it, Fenway," Patches says, nuzzling my neck.

Before I know it, a huge group of dogs stampedes over to us. One of them goes up to Lucky. "You were there, right? Did Fenway really fight off a pack of wolves?"

Lucky stands taller. "Ohmygosh! Ohmygosh!" he yips. "Fenway was amaaaaazing! You should've seen him!"

Before I can correct him, the Boston Terrier pipes up. "Hey, Fenway, wanna play chase?"

"I got here before you," says the Border Collie, nosing the Boston out of the way. "Play keep-away with me, Fenway. You can go first."

Hugo drops onto his forepaws. "How about showing us those moves on the climbing ramp, Fenway?" he asks, his bow tie flopping.

"Whatever you want!" Kwanzaa hops excitedly. "You're in charge, Fenway!" she says.

"For sure!" cries Titan the German Shepherd. "You tell us what to do, and we'll do it."

Midnight thumps her black, curly tail in agreement. Chorizo wags his tail, too.

I take a step back. "Whoa! Hang on, everybody." My head swivels around the Dog Park, from the giant water dish to the ramp to the crawling tube, but I don't see anyone with a sparkly collar. "Where's Coco?" I ask.

"Oh, that bossy little Pomeranian?" says one of the dogs. "I thought I saw her digging near the back fence."

"You don't have to worry about her," says another. "You're the leader now."

"That's just it," I say, before tearing out across the Dog Park. I don't slow down until I get to the back fence. Sure enough, Coco is sunk down in a small hole. As I stand over her, her dirty face pops up.

"What do you want now, *Fenway*?" she says in a disgusted voice. "Here to gloat?"

I cock my head. "I'm not even sure what that means. I came to ask you to help lead the games."

She looks surprised. "What did you say?"

"I'm all about having fun," I say, nudging her out of the hole. "And it's not fun being the leader all the time. At least not for me."

"Really?" she says. "You're not pulling my tail?"

"Definitely," I say. "As long as everybody gets to play. Even me."

Coco springs up on her paws. "Deal! Now, let's see if you can catch me!"

As she shoots out through the grass, I'm right behind her. The other dogs race over, and before I know it, we're all part of the Best Game of Chase Ever.

When most of the dogs have left the Dog Park, Hattie and Angel call me and the ladies over. Lucky and Coco trot along ahead of us. "Ohmygosh! Ohmygosh! Wasn't that fun, Coco?" Lucky says, panting.

"Sure was," Coco says, her collar glittering through her poofy fur.

Marcus and a couple of other boys are hanging by the gate. One of them is holding a fat ball. As the short humans clip on our leashes, Marcus comes up to Hattie, chattering. "Kick-ball?" I hear him say.

"Nah," Hattie says, exchanging a glance with June. Then she turns her painted cheek toward Marcus. "Like it?" she asks.

"Fair-ee??" When he grimaces, Hattie laughs. So does June. So does Angel. Hattie tucks her book under her arm, and we head out the gate.

Back at the clearing, all that's left of the campsite are the wooden tables, the Fire Spaces, and the cars. Which are as overloaded as they were when we first came here to the woods. "Ready, Fenway?" Hattie asks as we pile into the back seat. "See you in school!" she calls to the short humans, waving out the window.

There's that word again—"school." The place where short humans with backpacks go. And suddenly I get it—this is what all the changes are about. Hattie is going there again.

But she's excited. She's ready. And I know it will be okay.

As we drive away, I crawl onto Hattie's lap. I give her cheek a sloppy lick. She smells like paint and pine, but mostly like happiness.

I nuzzle into her shirt. Some changes might be scary. Some changes are all right. But loving Hattie is one thing that will stay the same. For always.

Acknowledgments

Every book has a story-behind-the-story.
This book has three.

1) In January 2017, then nine-year-old Olivia Van Ledtje invited me to record a "LivBit" with her at the launch party for *Fenway and Hattie and the Evil Bunny Gang*. Of course I agreed (even though I had yet to learn what a "LivBit" was). On camera, she suggested that I write a book where Fenway meets a Pomeranian named Coco. An idea was planted.

2) Later that year, my wise editor, Susan Kochan, suggested that Fenway and Hattie's family might go on a trip. The idea sprouted.

3) I thought of my own family's experiences with our dog, Kipper. The time he capsized our boat and lost our gear in the river. The time he drank so much seawater that he threw up on the beach. The time he "defended" our tent from anyone who walked by and nearly got us kicked out of the campground. These not-so-fond memories mashed up with the group camping tradition at my kids' elementary school. The idea bloomed. And the book practically wrote itself.

But writing is only the first step in a book's life, just as buying a tent is only the beginning of a camping trip. *Fenway and Hattie in the Wild* came about thanks to the help and support of many extraordinary professionals and friends.

A forest full of thanks to my agent, Marietta Zacker, for showing me the ropes. I cannot imagine this adventure without her as my trusted guide. And s'more thanks to the rest of the team at Gallt & Zacker. I feel so lucky to have these ladies in my camp.

Endless gratitude to my brilliant editor, Susan Kochan. Her kindness, wisdom, and professionalism are as big as the great outdoors.

A chorus of birdcalls for the rest of the team, especially Jamaica Ponder, for a fresh reading and fresh perspective; Wendy Dopkin, for cleaning up my messes; Trevor Ingerson, for making a splash with social media and the One School, One Book promotion; Susie Albert, for navigating trails to New England booksellers; Andrea Cruise, for planning and coordinating my classroom WRAD connections & beyond; Dave Kopka, for another tail-wagging cover and jacket; David Kreutz, for yet one more drool-worthy dog photo; and illustrator Kristine Lombardi, for the paw-some sketches at the head of each chapter.

Enormous thanks to my home base, the trusted readers of this story who kept me on the right path (and helped me find my way when I strayed): Bridget Hodder, Cheryl Lawton Malone, Theresa Milstein, Lisa J. Rogers, Elly Swartz, and Donna Woelki.

A bonfire of appreciation for librarian luminary Shannon Miller and her extremely enthusiastic students. Unveiling this book's fiery red cover with them was an experience I'll never forget.

Ranger hats off to all the dedicated educators and book nerds whose blogs and posts and real-life book talks have enabled the Fenway and Hattie series to trek into so many libraries, classrooms, and homes. I wish I could list everyone, but I want to give extra-special thanks to Margie Myers-Culver, Cynthia Merrill, Jason Lewis, John Schumacher, Donalyn Miller, Pernille Ripp, Michele Knott, Lesley Burnap, Rayna Freedman, Melanie Roy, Nikki Mancini, Becky Calzada, and Bobbi Hopkins. Their incredible guidance and generosity, particularly over this past year, was more than I could have ever imagined.

A round of campfire cheers for teacher Tracy Mitchell and her third graders of 2017–18 at East Clayton Elementary in Clayton, North Carolina, and Amanda Bonjour and her library full of students from Cody Elementary in Le Claire, Iowa, who named Titan the three-legged German Shepherd and Midnight the black Poodle, respectively. I can't wait for readers to meet these two aptly named characters!

If I could camp out anywhere in the world, it would be inside an independent bookstore. I'm so thankful for all the passionate booksellers who have helped get my books into the hands of readers. Special shout-outs to Peter H. Reynolds and Margie Leonard at The Blue Bunny, Kathy Detweiler and Bill Grace at Buttonwood Books, Lynnette at Henry Bear's Park, and Lisa Fabiano at An Unlikely Story, who regularly go the extra mile and beyond.

Mountains of thanks to the teachers, parents, and administrators of every elementary school I've visited this past year. Connecting with kids, particularly in a school setting, is an absolute honor and joy. To everyone who made those opportunities possible, you are the brightest stars in the night sky.

To my most cherished author buddies—Elly Swartz, Bridget Hodder, Cheryl Lawton Malone, and Lygia Day Penaflor—I would be truly lost without your love and friendship. You ladies are everything.

Kudos to my family, who are always ready to pitch in whenever I need anything. My amazing uncle Walter Swartz designed the Fenway cutout and the Books in the Kitchen logo, my brother Matthew Coe created two of the book trailers, and my son James Baker-Coe composed, performed, and recorded the music for all three trailers and also developed the *Fenway and Hattie* interactive game (victoriajcoe.com/play).

Lastly, love forever to my husband, Ralph, and my sons, Philip and James, who showed me the fun of camping—even if they say it's not real camping until someone complains!

Victoria J. Coe has survived exactly one camping trip with her dog, Kipper. In addition to writing books for children, she teaches creative writing to adults in Boston, where she and her family are always on the lookout for intruders.

www.victoriajcoe.com
Instagram.com/victoriajcoe
Twitter: @victoriajcoe

Find Fenway and Hattie activities for
home and classroom on Victoria J. Coe's Padlet:

padlet.com/victoriajcoe/FenwayAndHattieResources